Sam ... at a w ... only ... the planet.

Cassie reminded herself that he probably looked at every woman that way while he was with them, making each one of them feel special.

But telling herself that didn't seem to matter to her heart, which was beating faster than a journalist's heart should. A journalist's heart should be objective, interested in discovering the truth...not in discovering the feel of Sam's hands on her body.

Which brought her back to the fact that none of this was real.

Sam's interest in her wasn't real, because he didn't know the real her.

She was an impostor parading around as a confident whiplash-blonde, a tough chick. But inside she was the same out-of-step loner she'd always been.

For heaven's sake...she was still a virgin!

Dear Reader,

Now that the holidays are over, I'll bet you need some serious R and R, and what better way to escape the everyday and recharge your spirit than with Silhouette Romance? We'll take you on the rewarding, romantic journey from courtship to commitment!

This month you're in for some very special surprises! First, beloved Carolyn Zane returns with *The Cinderella Inheritance* (#1636), a tender, rollicking, triumphant rags-to-riches love story. Then Karen Rose Smith brings you the next installment in the amazing SOULMATES series. In *With One Touch* (#1638), Brooke Pennington can magically heal animals, but only Dr. Nate Stanton has the power to cure her own aching heart.

If the greatest lesson in life is love, then you won't want to miss these two Romance novels. In Susan Meier's *Baby on Board* (#1639), the first in her DAYCARE DADS miniseries, Caro Evans is hired to teach dark, guarded Max Riley how to care for his infant daughter—and how to love again. And in *The Prince's Tutor* (#1640) by Nicole Burnham, Amanda Hutton is used to instructing royal *children* about palace protocol, but not a full-grown playboy prince with other lessons in mind....

Appearances can be deceiving, especially in Cathie Linz's *Sleeping Beauty & the Marine* (#1637), about journalist Cassandra Jones who loses the glasses and colors her hair to find out if gentlemen prefer blondes, and hopes a certain marine captain doesn't! Then former bad-boy Matt Webster nearly goes bananas when he agrees to be the pretend fiancé of one irresistible virgin, in Shirley Jump's *The Virgin's Proposal* (#1641).

Next month, look for popular Romance author Carla Cassidy's 50th book, part of a duo called THE PREGNANCY TEST, about two women with two very different test results!

Happy reading!

Mary-Theresa Hussey

Mary-Theresa Hussey
Senior Editor

Please address questions and book requests to:
Silhouette Reader Service
U.S.: 3010 Walden Ave., P.O. Box 1325, Buffalo, NY 14269
Canadian: P.O. Box 609, Fort Erie, Ont. L2A 5X3

Sleeping Beauty & the Marine

CATHIE LINZ

SILHOUETTE *Romance*®

Published by Silhouette Books

America's Publisher of Contemporary Romance

For Heather and Jayne, romance divas
from the eHarlequin message boards.
Thanks for being there whenever I need you.

Acknowledgment
Special thanks to former marine "Sir" Bob Hill
for sharing his love of flying.

SILHOUETTE BOOKS

ISBN 0-373-19637-7

SLEEPING BEAUTY & THE MARINE

Visit Silhouette at www.eHarlequin.com

Printed in U.S.A.

CATHIE LINZ

left her career in a university law library to become a *USA TODAY* bestselling author of contemporary romances. She is the recipient of the highly coveted Storyteller of the Year Award given by *Romantic Times* and was recently nominated for a Love and Laughter Career Achievement Award for the delightful humor in her books.

Although Cathie loves to travel, she is always glad to get back home to her family, her various cats, her trusty computer and her hidden cache of Oreo cookies!

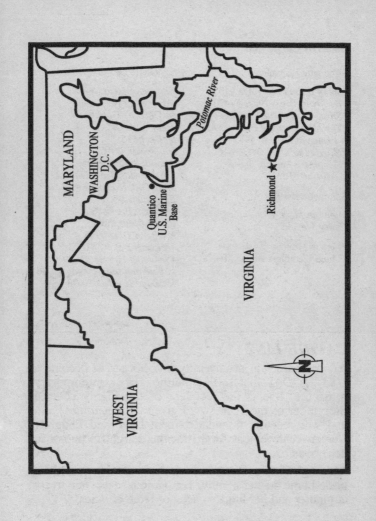

Chapter One

Payback time had come for U.S. Marine Captain Sam Wilder. And Cassandra Jones was just the woman to give it to him.

Watching him walk toward her, Cassie could see why he was so popular with women—with those blue eyes, chiseled features and dark hair, he was real nice eye candy.

"I'm sorry I was delayed, ma'am," Sam said as he joined her.

She noted the way his eyes gleamed with male appreciation as his gaze lingered on her. From her whip-lash-blond looks to her Tough Chick T-shirt, Cassandra Jones was a force to be reckoned with. This had not always been the case. Far from it.

But that was irrelevant now. She was here at Marine Corps Headquarters, Quantico, Virginia, for one reason and one reason only. Her career.

Cassie loved being a journalist. She loved the fact that her editor had enough confidence in her work to select her for such a high-profile feature series as "A Week in the Life of an American Hero." She didn't love the fact that the current American hero selected was U.S. Marine Captain Sam Wilder.

Although she was certain he had no memory of it, this actually wasn't the first time she and Sam had crossed paths, and the truth was that Cassie would rather chew glass than have to deal with him again. But she had to take the good with the bad in life. It was a lesson she'd learned as a small child and had never forgotten.

At that time there had often been more bad than good in her life. But things had changed since then. She was now an up-and-coming journalist with *Capital Magazine* and she had a job to do.

So here she was. Stuck with him. That didn't mean she had to be ecstatic about it, however. She'd been waiting almost half an hour for him to show up. "I thought Marines had a thing about being punctual."

Sam noted the slight hint of underlying hostility in her voice and wondered if this was another liberal left-wing reporter with a chip on her shoulder about the military. Sure, patriotism had come back into fashion lately, but that didn't mean that everyone had jumped on the bandwagon. And this woman definitely didn't look like someone who went along with the crowd.

The black slacks and white T-shirt she wore might have been conservative attire were it not for the glittery words Tough Chick strategically emblazoned across the cotton covering her breasts. Her blond hair framed her heart-shaped face and curved beneath her chin. She had an incredibly lush mouth and wide jungle-green eyes that reflected a certain amount of impatience.

Sam wasn't accustomed to a woman reacting this way to him. Usually their smiles reflected feminine appreciation or awareness or something...not impatience.

As the only remaining Wilder brother who was still a bachelor, Sam had taken his duties of continuing the family tradition of being a charmer as seriously as he took anything. While he was no womanizer, he had always been confident of his effect on the opposite sex. He'd never had to work at it before. The skill had simply been a part of him, like his blue eyes or dark hair.

This woman, however, showed no signs of being the least bit impressed...and that intrigued rather than irked him.

Sam had always been a man who enjoyed a challenge. In fact, after being stuck in Quantico instead of returning to active duty as he'd wanted, he was itching for a good challenge and a little excitement.

"We Marines do pride ourselves on punctuality, ma'am, among other things," he belatedly replied. "I was unavoidably detained." He gave her one of his trademark aw-shucks smiles that had always worked wonders on the female population in the past. "If I'd known such a lovely lady was waiting for me, I can assure you that I would have done everything in my power to get here faster."

"I'm sure you would have," Cassie drawled. She already knew from past experience that Sam paid attention to a woman's looks. "So how does it feel to be the Marine Corps's poster boy?"

"Excuse me?"

"Ever since you flew that surveillance mission and landed safely despite the fact that your plane had serious engine trouble, you've been hailed as an American hero, saving the lives of your crew."

"It was engine *failure,* not engine trouble, and I was just doing my job, ma'am."

"Come now, don't be modest. How does it feel having an entire country talking about you?"

"I doubt they're still talking about me. The incident to which you're referring occurred almost three months ago."

"Actually it was exactly two and a half months ago."

He narrowed his eyes. "You appear to have been counting the days. I wonder why that is?"

"A good reporter knows the facts." And the fact was that the press conference upon his return to the States had been a major event. One that she'd covered. Or attempted to. But she felt that Sam had ignored her attempts to have her questions answered, and had instead called on a pert blonde for his final question instead of her.

It was her photographer, Al, a grizzled pro of decades in the business, who had pointed out the fact that the blondes were the winners, getting all the attention, all the coverage. Feeling that Sam had looked right through her, ignored her waving hand, was the final straw. So she'd accepted Al's half-kidding dare for her to become a blonde.

Cassie had been tired of being ignored, of being the quiet brunette with the tiny-framed smart-girl glasses who'd never been called on in high school, who'd been overlooked in college, who was continuously trying to get her editor Phil to give her a chance at some of the bigger stories for the past six months only to be told her time would come.

Someone who came from a regular middle-class background might believe that. Might still believe in happy endings. But Cassie knew better. She believed in making your own luck.

Her earliest memory was of being hungry, of her mother lying on the couch with a bottle of liquor on the floor beside her. Her mother never meant to get drunk again. Something or someone else had always caused it. The blame always started with Cassie's father, who'd died when she was a baby, leaving her mother alone to cope. "Your father left us," she used to say, as if he'd died in a car accident on purpose, just to make her mother's life miserable.

As the years went by, Cassie had quickly learned to be the responsible one, the one who bought the groceries from what was left of her mother's meager waitress salary. Her mother had a bad habit of buying alcohol first. They'd moved often, skipping out in the middle of the night when they lacked the money to pay the rent, and they often went without electricity or a phone.

Cassie had started working when she was fifteen but she'd always made sure to study hard, realizing that an education was her ticket out. She wasn't about to let a man derail her the way her mother had been derailed by Cassie's father's death. In those days Cassie had hid her vulnerability beneath a quietly serious exterior.

After her mother's death when Cassie was eighteen, she'd gone to Northwestern on an academic scholarship. She'd had to work hard, studying late into the night and working part-time jobs to make ends meet.

She'd kept her nose to the grindstone, and got a job as an intern for a suburban newspaper in the Chicago area. That led to a job with the paper, which led to another job with another bigger paper, and so on and so on until she'd come to Washington, D.C. to work for *Capital Magazine* six months ago.

She'd covered Sam's press conference that day because the normal reporter had been out sick. Cassie had been so filled with hope; hope that her editor would finally notice her work. Instead she'd left with nothing new to report and a determination to make a change in her life.

She'd been sitting back, waiting for opportunity to come knocking on her door. She'd made a vow that day to be the one doing the knocking, not the one waiting around.

Cassie had gone right from that disastrous press conference directly to a ritzy salon with only one request. ''Make me blond.''

Her desire for change had had nothing to do with catching the attention of such a sexy man as Sam Wilder. No, it had everything to do with *power*. She was tired of being overlooked. She wanted to get ahead in her career. She wanted the power.

Cassie was tough, she'd learned early that the only person you could depend on was yourself. She might have been quiet, but that didn't mean she was a doormat. She'd moved to Washington, D.C., to start a new life and changing her appearance had just been the next step in the process. She wanted to be a woman who took risks.

The colorist at the salon, a tall bald man named Ivan, was the one who'd come up with the term ''whiplash blonde,'' referring to the fact that by the time he was done with her, she'd turn heads. She could still remember waking up the next morning and wondering who the strange woman reflected in her bathroom mirror was...before realizing it was her.

Al had been right. Blondes did get noticed. And Ivan had been right. She was now a whiplash blonde. Since changing her hair color, and discarding her black-rimmed glasses for contacts, her boss had taken more notice of her writing, finally giving Cassie the chance she'd been waiting for. She wasn't about to blow it now.

"A good reporter knows the facts, hmm?" Sam repeated. "So does a good Marine."

"You still haven't answered my initial question," she reminded him, her pen poised over her notepad. "How does it feel to be the Marine Corps's poster boy? Do you have any regrets that young teenage boys are lining up to join the Marines because of you, because you became a national celebrity?"

"I sense a certain hostility on your part. Care to tell me why that is?"

"I think you're being too sensitive, Sam."

His jaw tightened. "Marines aren't sensitive, Cassie."

She didn't like him calling her that. Cassie was her past, Cassandra was her present. "My name is Cassandra."

"And my name is Sam, not 'poster boy.' If my actions help the Marine Corps and my country, then that's fine by me. I don't go looking for attention."

She frowned at him. Was that supposed to be some kind of crack at her? Was he somehow insinuating that she was the one looking for attention?

No, there was no way he could know she'd colored

her hair and changed her appearance. Now she was the one being too sensitive.

"Why did you decide to write this story?" Sam demanded.

"Because my boss told me to," she answered honestly.

He nodded as if something had just clicked into place for him. "The same reason I'm here to be interviewed. Because I've been ordered to. So why don't we both make the best of a bad situation and continue this over dinner."

"Dinner?" she repeated blankly. Two months ago the guy looked right through her at his press conference and now he wanted her to go out with him?

"Dinner. As in evening meal. You do eat, don't you?"

"Yes, but…"

"Then we might as well be enjoying a meal. I know a great Thai place not far away. So what do you say?"

"It will take longer than one dinner to finish my story about you."

Sam grinned, his dark blue eyes gleaming with sexy humor, a dimple appearing in one lean cheek. "Well, ma'am, I'd be willing to put myself at your disposal for as long as it takes."

"Good," she said briskly. "I was hoping you'd say that. Because I plan on being your shadow for the next week or two."

His expression turned cautious. "What does that mean exactly?"

"It means that *Capital Magazine* is doing a series of articles entitled 'A Week in the Life of an American Hero.' The last subject of my story was a fireman. Now it's a Marine. You. My job is to stick like glue, to figure out what makes you tick, to be a fly on the wall of your life.''

"You don't look like a fly, more like a butterfly.''

"Butterflies are wimps,'' she scoffed.

"I was under the impression that you'd be interviewing me today and that would be it.''

"You were under the wrong impression.''

"Has this been cleared…?''

"It certainly has,'' she interrupted him. "From the highest level of the Marine Corps. I'm surprised your commanding officer didn't tell you that.''

Sam wasn't surprised. The truth was he hadn't paid that much attention when his C.O. had told him about this interview. Sam had assumed that it would be like the other interviews he'd done over the course of the past few weeks.

He should have known that nothing about Cassandra Jones was business as usual. She was definitely one of a kind.

"In that case, we should go have dinner. I'll drive and we'll discuss the schedule while we eat.''

"Sam, I hate to break this to you, but I'm not in the Marines.''

Eyeing her T-shirt, he murmured, "I did notice that, ma'am.''

Cassie felt her cheeks grow hot, a first for her. She wasn't the kind who embarrassed easily. Not lately, anyway. "And since I'm not a Marine, I'd appreciate it if you didn't order me around as if I were one.''

"Sorry. Hazard of the job, ma'am.''

She wanted to ask him about the other hazards of his job, about his reasons for becoming a Marine, about his ways of dealing with the dangers he faced.

But she was smart enough to know that he'd be more relaxed over dinner and she might get more candid answers out of him in that case.

Which was the only reason she accepted Sam's invitation to dinner. Not because of his cute grin, his muscular body, or his incredible blue eyes. And not because he managed to look good in his khaki service uniform, which was a shade of green that didn't normally look good on anyone. But it looked good on him. She suspected he'd look sexy in just about anything, or in nothing at all.

Great. Ten minutes in the guy's company and already she was starting to have sexual fantasies about him. Not a good sign.

"Give me directions to the restaurant and I'll meet you there," she said.

"I thought you were supposed to be my shadow," Sam noted.

"Fine, we'll both go in my car. Unless you have a thing about being in the driver's seat all the time?"

"I'm willing to let a woman who knows what she wants take control every now and then."

The husky way he said the words made her think he was talking about making love rather than driving to a restaurant. If the man was trying to throw her, he was in for a surprise.

"I'm so glad to hear that," she purred as they headed out for the parking lot. "I like a man who knows when to sit back and go with the flow."

His humorous gaze was now laced with an element of admiration. At first she thought he was gazing at her, but then she decided he must be eyeing her fire-engine-red Miata.

"Buckle up." She grinned as she slid into the driver's seat. "You're in for the ride of your life."

"Have you ever heard of a brake?" Sam said twenty minutes later. "A useful thing, it's the pedal right next to the gas."

"You're putting fingerprints on my dashboard," she reprimanded him. "I never thought you'd be a white-knuckle passenger. Not a daredevil Marine like you."

"I'm not a daredevil," Sam denied through gritted teeth. "I know what I'm doing. I don't take unnecessary risks."

"Too bad. I take them all the time these days," she admitted with a grin. "You see, I've finally discovered that if you don't take risks you'll never succeed."

"You take any more risks and we won't make it to the restaurant alive."

She eased up on the gas.

He leaned back in his seat and eyed her with speculation. "Was this some kind of test? A way of seeing if you could freak out the big bad Marine?"

She was surprised by his question. "You're a hero. Why would I try to freak out a hero?"

"You tell me."

"I wasn't trying to freak you out. I was just enjoying a little freedom." Her mouth clamped shut as if she regretted saying as much as she had.

Sam watched her in the mellow twilight. She was a study of contradictions. That wide mouth outlined in cherry-red spoke of a sensual woman. And while her T-shirt proclaimed that she was a Tough Chick, he'd seen the way she'd patted the roof of her car before getting into it, almost as if it were a favored pet. He'd also noticed the way she'd stopped longer at a stop sign to let an elderly woman walk across. She might talk tough, but he had a feeling there was more to Cassandra Jones than met the eye.

Not that what met the eye wasn't pretty darn sexy. She was definitely a woman you noticed.

She turned heads as they walked into the restaurant. She'd added a tailored black jacket that hid the Tough Chick writing on her T-shirt, but there was no hiding the fact that she was a confident and attractive woman. It was there in the way she walked, hips sashaying like poetry in motion.

The Thai place had an unassuming atmosphere with several tapestries hanging from the whitewashed walls. Pristine-white tablecloths adorned the light birchwood tables. The matching chairs had colorfully upholstered seats, adding dashes of vibrancy to the otherwise austere surroundings. Cassie's black chunky heels clinked on the hardwood floor as they were led to a table in the corner.

It wasn't until she opened her menu that Sam noticed the tattoo near her wrist. The long sleeve of her jacket pulled back momentarily, showing him a flash of something...a tiny heart maybe?

Noticing his attention, she said, "Yes, it's a tattoo. I had it done when I was a teenager."

"To remind you of your first love?"

"To remind me never to wear my heart on my sleeve," she retorted.

Spoken like a Tough Chick. But Sam saw something in her green eyes, a flash of pain that was there and gone. He knew better than to press her. He focused on the food instead.

"Some of the dishes here are pretty spicy..." he began.

"I like spicy," she said. "The hotter the better."

"Really?" He quirked an eyebrow at her. "Their Pad Khing really isn't for wimps. And their Crying Tiger has made grown men cry. Maybe you should have some nice spring rolls—"

"Puh-lease," she interrupted him. "Do I look like a wimp? I can take anything they dish up. What about you?"

Sam could feel his competitive juices flowing. This woman challenged him on so many unexpected levels. She was even turning a meal into a contest.

He liked it.

He liked her.

This could turn out to be much more interesting than he'd anticipated.

"I can take whatever *anyone* dishes up," Sam stated.

"I'll keep that in mind."

"You do that. So what are you ordering?"

"I'm trying to decide between the Crying Tiger with the beef and homemade hot sauce or the Pad Khing Thai-style. What about you?"

"I'm definitely having the Crying Tiger," Sam told the waitress who had just come to take their order. "But it may be too much for you," he added for Cassandra's benefit.

"I doubt that. I'll have Crying Tiger, too," Cassandra said.

"It is very, very spicy," the waitress warned her.

"Good." Cassandra handed her the menu.

Sam waited until the waitress left before resuming their conversation.

"So tell me about yourself. How long have you been a journalist?"

"I'm the one interviewing you," she reminded him as she took a sip of ice water.

Sam watched as she licked away a drop of water from her lips. His body tightened. She had the kind of mouth that could lead a man into battle. He couldn't remember the last time a woman had had this kind of instantly powerful effect on him.

"So, Sam, why the Marines? Why not the Army or the Air Force?"

"Because the Marines are the best."

"At what?"

"At everything."

"Really?" She raised an eyebrow. "At everything?"

"That's right, ma'am."

"At cooking and doing dishes?"

"In so far is it applies to our operations, then yes, even at cooking and doing dishes."

"I'd heard that Marines were a confident bunch."

"You heard correctly, ma'am."

"I've also heard about the Marine Corps's esprit de corps. Would you care to give me an example of that?"

"Certainly. Take tattoos."

She blinked. "Tattoos?"

He nodded. "When sailors get tattoos they choose something to express their individuality, like Mickey Mouse or a raging sea serpent or any one of a dozen other things. When we Marines get tattoos we do it to express our solidarity."

"No Mickey Mouses or raging sea serpents?"

He shook his head and rolled up his sleeve. "We

select 'Death Before Dishonor,' the Marine Corps mascot of a bulldog, or simply U.S.M.C.''

"I see you went with the simple U.S.M.C. yourself.'' She nodded at his tattoo, while also noting the muscular shape of his arm. There was no way her mouth had gone dry simply because he'd shown her his tattoo. No, she was just thirsty. She reached for her glass of ice water again.

Time to regain control of this interview. "Do you have the same kind of rivalry with your three older brothers that you seem to have with the rest of the branches of the armed services?''

She could tell by the flash of surprise in his blue eyes that she'd scored a direct hit.

He recovered quickly, however. "Marines are a naturally competitive bunch, ma'am,'' he drawled. "You might want to remember that the next time you hand out a challenge. You might end up getting more than you bargained for.''

"I can handle whatever you care to dish out,'' she instantly retorted.

"We'll just have to see about that, now won't we?''

"Yes, we will.'' Too bad she no longer felt quite as confident as she sounded.

He gave her a slow smile sexy enough to melt the sternest female heart. "I have the feeling we're about to embark on a very interesting journey together. So fasten your seat belt, Cassie. You may be in for the ride of your life.''

Chapter Two

"Too hot for you?" Sam inquired.

Cassie had barely recovered her composure from Sam's husky proclamation that she was in for the ride of her life when their waitress brought their meals. She'd taken one bite of her Crying Tiger and now it felt as if her tongue were on fire. No, not just her tongue...her entire mouth and throat. Tears sprang to her eyes although she quickly blinked them away.

"Too hot for you?" he repeated.

"No." Her voice sounded husky. Probably because her vocal cords had been singed. "What about you?" she countered.

"What about me?"

"I saw the way you reached for your glass of beer."

"And what way was that?"

"Desperate. The way someone reaches for water to put out a flame."

"I was merely thirsty."

"Me, too." She grabbed for her own tall, cold glass of imported beer.

"So, is the food spicy enough for you?"

"It will do."

"I thought it was a little on the mild side myself."

"Mmm, it *is* a little mild," she lied.

"We could ask for more of their homemade hot sauce."

"We could. Do you want to?"

"Do you?" Sam countered.

She recognized a challenge when presented with one. "Sure. Why not?"

Once the additional spicy sauce was added, she waited until Sam took a bite before taking one of her own. Her eyes watered even more, but then so did his. She felt vindicated.

"That's better." His voice was raspy. "Still a little mild, though."

She had to laugh. "I might be more inclined to believe that statement were it not for the smoke coming out of your ears."

He grinned at her. "So I guess it's a tie then."

"What is?"

"The Spicy Food Contest."

"I did tell you that hot and spicy is my specialty."

"I tend to have a weakness for hot…and spicy myself." His voice was husky and his pauses deliberate.

"I was referring to the food."

"So was I." His expression was innocent enough, but the gleam in his deep blue eyes didn't fool her for one minute.

The Marine poster boy was flirting with her. Tempting as it was, she refused to flirt back. The mere fact that she wanted to was an indication that she felt more than she should for this confident flyboy.

She had no intention of being one of the many women who drooled over him. A Tough Chick never drooled…unless it was over a two-pound box of Godiva dark chocolate truffles. And even then, only a little drool was allowed. While she was still new at this Tough Chick stuff, she was pretty confident that drooling was a no-no. Showed too much vulnerability. And hiding her inner vulnerability was something she was a pro at doing after all these years.

"If the food is too much for you, you don't have to finish it all," Sam said as if granting her a huge favor.

"Are you kidding? It's delicious." She took another bite to prove her point. By now her mouth was beginning to grow numb from the overstimulation of her taste buds. The truth was, she did love spicy food.

"Delicious," he repeated, his attention focused on her mouth.

The Marine was good, she'd grant him that. His charm was as powerful as the fiery meal.

He'd also recovered surprisingly quickly to her earlier attempts to throw him by asking him why he'd joined the Marines. But it was still early in the process. She suspected he had yet to fully understand the true requirements of this article.

"We should discuss your schedule." Her voice was all business now. "As I said earlier, I'm doing a series of articles about the life of an American hero. That means I'll be your shadow."

"A fly on the wall of my life was the way you put it earlier, if I recall correctly."

"You do," she confirmed.

"That sounds all very well and good under normal circumstances, but you have to realize that I don't have a normal nine-to-five job at an office. Yes, I'm temporarily assigned to Marine headquarters here, but I'm waiting for new orders."

"You'd rather be flying planes than stuck here in Washington."

"Your words, not mine."

Sam wasn't about to give her anything she could use against him. He could just see the headline now: Marine Poster Boy Hates Being Stuck In Washington.

No, he wasn't about to give her any ammunition.

"Then put it in your own words," she suggested.

"Put what in my words?"

"How you feel about being stuck in Washington, so far away from the action."

"The Marine Corps feels this is the best place for me to be at this time. A good Marine doesn't question his orders."

"You never question your orders?"

"Not if they are lawful orders, no."

"It's been said that the definition of a hero is an ordinary person who is called upon through circumstances beyond his control to do extraordinary things. How does that apply to your situation?"

"I've already said that I was just doing my job. Nothing I did was extraordinary. It's something we train for, something we have to be prepared for."

"Funny. I interviewed an area firefighter who was called to the Pentagon when it was hit and he said the same thing. That he was just doing his job, what he'd been trained to do..." She paused to scribble some notes on the white paper tablecloth.

"Don't you have a notebook or something to write on?" he asked.

"I left it in the car." She finished writing her train of thought before looking up. "We still need to discuss the schedule."

"I don't think you realize what you're getting into here."

"Really?" Cassie retorted. "Well, then that's something we have in common. Because I don't think *you* realize what *you're* getting into. The requirements of this article are such that I'll need access to your days and part of your evenings. I realize the latter might put a crimp in your social life, so I'm willing to work around whatever private time you might need in respect to that."

"What are you talking about?"

"A hot date."

He appeared to be delighted. "You're asking me out on a hot date?"

"No way."

"Why 'no way'?"

"Because you're the subject of my story. What I meant was that if you have any hot dates scheduled for these next two weeks, I'll work around them so that you can continue on with…whatever."

"How generous of you," Sam noted wryly. "I don't have any hot dates lined up, however."

"No?" She would have thought his social calendar would be filled with one date after another. She could easily picture him with some adoring cheerleader type, someone who'd hang on his every word while hanging on his arm like a limpet.

"No, not at the moment. However I do have some other commitments."

"Like what?"

"Like a charity event at the Willard Hotel tomorrow night. You should definitely come with me for that."

"You weren't planning on going with someone else?"

"No, I was going stag. Why? Is the idea of working fourteen hours a day too tough for you?"

"Fourteen-hour days are a piece of cake," she scoffed. Charity events were another matter, though. No one did events like Washington socialites. And the Willard, with its turn-of-the-century Crystal Room, was *the* preferred site for glittering galas. She sighed. "I suppose it's a formal affair."

He nodded. "You don't look too pleased about it."

"Getting all dressed up, wearing tight shoes, eating rubbery chicken, trying to make polite conversation with people who could care less what you say... Oh, yeah. That's definitely my idea of a good time," she noted sarcastically.

"Mine, too."

His smile was contagious. She found herself getting distracted by his good looks until she caught herself. "Tell me more about your schedule. How and when do you begin your day?"

"I start out with a two- or three-mile run every morning. You don't have to join me for that," Sam added.

"Sure I do."

"You might not be able to keep up with me," he warned her.

"Let me worry about that."

"I suppose I could slow down..." he said.

The concept of him making concessions hit a sore

point with her, reminding her of her childhood when other kids would look at her shabby clothes with pity. "Hey, there's no need to do me any favors. I said I can keep up with you."

"Are you a runner?"

She shrugged. "I've done my share of running in my time."

"Which means no."

"It means I can run as fast as you can."

"You sure are a competitive little thing, aren't you?"

She narrowed her eyes at him dangerously. "You might want to rephrase that comment."

"You have a great deal of competitive spirit. Do you like that better?"

"There's nothing wrong with being competitive."

"Nothing at all," Sam agreed. "It makes life interesting."

"Among other things. So you start out your day running. Where?"

"On one of the tracks at Quantico."

"What time?"

"Oh six hundred."

"Which is what, six in the morning?"

"That's right. Is that a problem for you?"

"No, of course not." She rarely got to sleep before one in the morning, but who needed sleep anyway. "What comes next on your schedule?"

"I shower and dress for work."

"You're on your own for that segment," she quickly informed him. "Then what?"

"Every day is different. At the moment I'm temporarily working with P.A.O.—the Public Affairs Office. They deal with internal and external information as well as ComRel—Community Relations. The office sets up my schedule. For example, tomorrow night I'm attending the charity event in an official capacity. It makes for a very long day."

"I can handle it. I'm as tough as you are."

His expression was clearly disbelieving.

"You don't believe me?" she demanded.

"I believe you think you're tough. But as tough as I am? No," he said bluntly. "There's no way you're as tough as I am. Think about it. I've had years of training, intense physical training on which I'm annually tested to confirm my fitness as a Marine."

"Toughness isn't all physical."

"I agree. A large part is mental, as well. I'm sure you're tough in your own way."

She would have let him off the hook had he not added that last condescending statement. "In my own way? And what way might that be? Some kind of inferior dainty-girl way?"

"No, in a Tough Chick kind of way."

"Inferior to a Marine Corps kind of way, however."

"Affirmative."

"We'll just see about that, buddy. We'll just see who outruns who on the track tomorrow morning."

The next morning, Cassie kept her sunglasses on as she walked onto the outdoor track. The day was overcast but that didn't matter. Indigestion from the overly spicy food had kept her up for most of the night. Her stomach was still a bit queasy and frankly the idea of running right now was not very appealing.

Not that any of her misgivings showed. At least, she hoped they didn't. She'd taken care to make sure they didn't. The black jogging shorts and top made her look like someone who knew what they were doing. She'd bought them when she'd joined the local health club before realizing she didn't have time to run around for no reason. Running to catch a bus, yes, but just running? No. She let her membership lapse and the jogging outfit had remained tossed in the back of her jumbled closet. Until this morning.

"Good morning." Sam's voice was so cheerful she wanted to throttle him.

Her greeting was not as bubbly. In fact, it resembled a murmured grumble.

Sam smiled. "Not a morning person, huh?"

Cassie grunted and guzzled more coffee from the huge paper cup she'd brought with her. When it was gone, she almost weeped. She needed more caffeine. Maybe there was a vending machine nearby and she could get some soda.

But no, no time for that. Mr. Cheerful was peeling off his sweatshirt, revealing a black T-shirt with U.S.M.C. on it. The short sleeves ended just above the U.S.M.C. tattoo on his left arm and the material clung to his muscular chest.

Hey, if it was material clinging to a chest he wanted, she could play that game, too. She unzipped her jogging jacket to reveal the spandex top she wore beneath it.

He paused to look at her. "I think you have that top on backward," he said. "There's a label sticking out of the neck."

"It's supposed to be there." She reached up and ripped the offending label off. "There, now are you happy?"

"Sure. Let's get started with some warming up exercises first."

"Warming up?" She was hot enough as it was, especially after seeing him looking all athletic and sexy.

"Affirmative. It prevents injuries. I thought we'd begin by taking a couple of laps around the track at a slow pace in order to allow you to gradually warm up."

He was using that condescending voice again, the one that drove her crazy. "I told you that you didn't have to make special accommodations for my running with you."

"I'm just using common sense. You have nothing against common sense, do you?"

"Depends whose version of common sense you're talking about. My version may be entirely different than yours."

"Are you ready to get started?"

"Absolutely." She was sort of jiggling around in place, her version of warming up. It had worked for her very successfully the last time she'd run, during the Why Me Breast Cancer 5K Run a year ago.

Sam gave her a cautionary look. "Nothing fast, remember."

She nodded. "Sure, I remember."

"Nice and slow."

"Somehow I never associated those two words with the Marine Corps," she retorted.

His laugh was deep and warm. "Depends what your assignment is." His strong masculine voice had a husky pitch that gave her goose bumps. "Certain activities require you to go nice and very slow in order to ensure successful…completion."

She had the definite feeling that he was talking about sex. Or maybe it was just her. Since seeing him in his black running shorts and T-shirt she'd had a hormone meltdown.

Or maybe it was a caffeine withdrawal. She hadn't had enough coffee this morning, that had to be it. She much preferred that diagnosis than the possibility that Sam Wilder was getting to her.

"Enough talking," she said, blaming her breathlessness on her warmup and not on Sam. "Let's get going, shall we?"

"Sure. I'll let you set the pace."

"Okay." It wasn't until Cassie had run halfway around the track that it occurred to her that by running behind her, Sam was getting a very good view of her derriere. Not her best feature. Suddenly it felt as big as a house. A jiggly house.

She stopped and turned to face him.

He almost ran smack into her.

Sam put his hands on her shoulders to prevent their collision.

"Why did you stop?" he demanded with a frown.

"I decided that you should go first."

"What?" He looked at her as if she were one pancake short of a full stack.

"You should run in front of me," she said.

"Why?" he demanded suspiciously.

"Why does there have to be a reason?"

"You're a woman," he immediately retorted. "There's always a reason."

"That's a chauvinistic thing to say."

"Fine, if you want me to run first I will." He took off.

She closely followed him the rest of the way around the track before wondering if she hadn't put herself into an even more volatile situation. Because now she was watching him and his magnificent form. She soon became fascinated by the interplay of rippling muscles from his calves, up to his thighs, and higher...

"Enjoying the view?" he taunted over his shoulder.

"Nothing worth looking at," Cassie retorted before sprinting past him. Maybe if she got enough ahead of him he wouldn't notice her derriere. But he immediately caught up with her. Now they were jogging side by side.

Out of the corner of her eye she could see his muscular arms. He had wonderful arms, not hairy. They were tanned and reminded her of a work of art—not too brawny, just right. What would it be like to be held in those arms? To feel them tightening around her?

She looked down. Now her own breasts were in her line of vision. Thank heavens she'd worn a sports bra. The lingerie was supposed to stop you from bouncing. But now that her attention was focused there, she realized she *was* bouncing. With every step she ran.

She shot a look over at Sam. Yep, he was watching her bouncing. His gaze wasn't lascivious, but it was hot and sexy. She almost stumbled over her own two feet before recovering her balance.

"You okay?" he asked.

"Fine." She ran a little faster.

He kept up with her.

She ran a little slower.

He matched her pace.

She had no idea how many laps they'd completed when he finally said, "Last lap."

She could only nod, lacking sufficient oxygen or energy at that point to even speak.

When they finally came to a stop, she just wanted

to fall into a heap. Instead he put her through a series of stretching exercises, from top to bottom. He started with neck stretches and shoulder stretches all the way down to shin and foot stretches. At first she suspected he was trying to ogle certain parts of her anatomy again by making her do these contortions, but then she decided he simply wanted to torture her by stretching her to death.

Even worse was the fact that Sam looked incredibly sexy with his skin gleaming with sweat as he wrapped a towel around his neck and tilted his head back to drink from his water bottle. She, on the other hand, felt as limp as a dishrag.

"Time to hit the showers," he cheerfully announced.

"Oh, joy," she muttered, secretly longing for her own shower at home with its variable massage settings.

Ten minutes later Cassie had completed her shower and her internal pep talk. Okay, she'd survived the first two hurdles—the jogging and the shower. So far, so good. The Marine hadn't thrown anything her way that she couldn't handle.

She was strong. She was woman, hear her roar. She was a whiplash-blond Tough Chick. She could do this. She could write this story without falling victim to Sam's charms. She would come out of this situation stronger and wiser. She would not fail. She would not drool. She would not allow him to see the inner Cassie that she hid from the rest of the world. She would not follow in her mother's footsteps and fall for a smooth-talking charmer. She would not allow herself to love so obsessively that she lost all sense of self-worth and direction as her mother had after Cassie's father's death.

Cassie checked her appearance in the mirror hanging above the row of sinks. She was wearing one of her power outfits—black pants and boots with a fitted red jacket. The required ID badge hung from a chain around her neck with her name, photo and the word Press.

Cassie had long ago vowed she'd make her own way in this life, she'd pursue her own dreams of becoming a well-known and respected journalist. And she wouldn't let anyone stand in her way, she wouldn't let anyone tempt her from her goal.

So, let the sexy Marine give her his best shot. She was a whiplash-blond Tough Chick now. She could handle it. She could handle him.

She just needed a little more coffee first....

Chapter Three

The Marine was trying to kill her. There was no other way of looking at it.

Oh, sure he was devious in his approach. Nothing obvious like doing her in on the track or attacking her in the shower.

No, he was much more subtle than that.

The Marine was trying to kill her...with boredom. It was all Cassie could do not to fall asleep as she sat in a chair in a boxlike office filled with cubicles and watched as Sam Wilder replaced one file with another.

He was doing it on purpose. She was sure of it. He was playing mind games with her, thinking that if he was dull enough she'd leave him alone.

News flash. That wasn't gonna happen.

She really should just sit here and enjoy the view. Not that there was a window in her line of vision. Instead she was in the bowels of a maze of cubicles, one looking pretty much the same as the other.

The cubicle she and Sam were in had a gray metal

desk, a swivel chair he was sitting in, and a straight-back chair she was occupying. She'd already counted the floor tiles beneath her feet, the folders on the desk, the pencils in the U.S.M.C. pencil holder.

She'd already written down an outline for her story structure and a list of questions she wanted to ask him. But he'd told her that he had to get rid of this paperwork before he could answer any questions, and the sooner he did that, the sooner they could get on with things.

Given the small confines of the cubicle, Cassie had to look at Sam. She kept noticing little things, such as the sweep of his dark lashes against his cheek. They matched his dark brows, making his intense blue eyes even more startling. Tiny laugh lines fanned out from the corner of his eyes even though he looked very serious as he gave all his attention to the paperwork and computer screen in front of him. He typed like a five-year-old, using the hunt-and-peck routine, but then no one was perfect.

He'd exchanged his jogging clothes for his uniform. Ah, his uniform. She should get the details on that for her article. She was pretty sure it was a service uniform but she wanted to confirm that.

"What do you call your uniform?" she asked him, tapping him on the arm to get his attention.

"I don't call my uniform anything." He hit the backspace again to delete a typo.

"What kind of uniform is it?"

"A Marine Corps uniform, ma'am."

"You're trying to drive me crazy, aren't you? Well, better men than you have tried and failed."

He quirked an eyebrow at her as if to say *Really? Tell me about it.* But she wasn't about to be distracted.

"I need the specific details about your uniform so that I can describe it correctly in my article," she explained.

"It's a service uniform."

"Fine. A service uniform. The shirt is khaki and the pants are darker...olive maybe?"

"Colors aren't my thing, ma'am."

She noticed he'd been ma'aming her since they'd entered the building. She suspected it was part of the treatment intended to drive her crazy, therefore she ignored it. Instead she said, "So what is your thing, Captain?"

"The Marine Corps, ma'am. And flying."

"Ah, flying. Tell me more about that. Tell me about flying."

"What would you like to know?"

"Why you became a pilot?"

"Because I like to fly." Presumably noticing the way her jaw was clenched in frustration at his vague answers, he said, "Did you need anything, ma'am? A drink perhaps? You appear to be grinding your teeth as if you were in need of liquid refreshment."

She immediately relaxed her jaw and fixed him with an exasperated glare. "Do you often have this effect on women?" What had made her say that? She clenched her teeth again. At least it prevented her from saying something she shouldn't.

"What affect might that be, ma'am?"

Okay, the Marine was having entirely too much fun taunting her. Time to turn the tables on him. "Tell me about the women in your life, Captain."

"The women?"

"That's right. I believe you were listed in an area newspaper as one of D.C.'s most eligible bachelors.

I'm sure the women have flocked to you since you've been declared a hero.''

What could Sam say, that they'd flocked to him even before that? While it was true, it didn't sound very good. He'd never been one to draw attention to himself that way. It wasn't the Marine thing to do. When you joined the Corps, you traded the word *me* for *we*. This group philosophy had actually been in-grained in him since he'd been born into a family of Marines.

There had never been any doubt that he, too, would become a Marine. At least there had never been any doubt in anyone else's mind.

He frowned. Where had that thought come from?

Sam turned to face Cassie. She was the one who'd gotten him all stirred up…in every way possible. Now she was asking him about the ''women'' in his life, as if he were some kind of Warrior Casanova, which left *him* grinding *his* teeth in frustration.

She was doing it on purpose, of course. Probably to punish him for making her sit here all morning while he pushed papers. Even so, he couldn't let her know that now she was pushing his buttons.

He was attempting to deal with her the way he dealt with any other mission, by applying the same four-step mental process he'd learned in Officer Training School here at Quantico. He began with observation, then orientation, decision and action.

During this initial observation phase he'd come to know a number of things about Cassie Jones—that she had a strong will, that her jungle-green eyes flashed with her emotions, that she was competitive and capable, that she wasn't easily charmed, that she made him weak in the knees when she ran by his side, that she nibbled her luscious lower lip when she was writing notes, that she intrigued him.

"You were going to tell me about the women in your life," Cassie reminded him.

"My private life really isn't that interesting, ma'am. I'm done here." He closed the last file. "Are you ready for a tour of the rest of the facility?"

"Sure." She'd let him off the hook this time. There would be time enough to cover that territory later. Like tonight. This charity event wasn't something she was exactly looking forward to. It tapped into too many of her own personal insecurities. "So, this thing tonight, uh…it's formal you said?"

"That's right. Would you like me to pick you up?"

She nodded absently, her mind on what she'd be wearing. It wasn't as if she had a bevy of ballgowns hanging in her closet just waiting for her to select one of them.

While one part of her mind listened to what Sam said as he gave her the brief history of the Marine Corps, another part was nibbling away at her recently boosted self-confidence.

Who was she kidding? Outwardly she might look like a whiplash-blond Tough Chick but inwardly she was still the same insecure girl who'd gone to bed every night praying that her mother would stop drinking and learn to love her.

"Was I talking too fast for you?" Sam asked.

"What?"

"I saw that you weren't taking any notes and I wondered if I was talking too fast."

"No. I've already gathered research on the Marine Corps's illustrious history."

"What about here at Quantico? Do you know the history of this place?"

"I know that it's called the 'Crossroads of the Marine Corps,' located on approximately one hundred square miles along the western bank of the Potomac River. It became a Marine Corps base in 1917."

"You've got the statistics down pat," he acknowledged. "But how about the concept?"

"The concept?"

Sam nodded. "Quantico isn't just a Marine Corps base. It's the heart of the Marine Corps. Today's Marine Corps University is where most Marine officers begin their careers and many enlisted men keep up with their military education. Quantico has served as the birthing place for combat concepts and ideas that are crucial to our continued success. The Marine Corps motto is *Semper Fidelis,* which means Always Faithful. The motto for Quantico is *Semper Progredi* or Always Forward."

There was no mistaking the pride in Sam's voice when he spoke about his beloved Marine Corps. Even his body language reflected his feelings. His military stance—shoulders erect, head held high—exuded a natural sense of power. Add that to his good looks and it made for a very attractive package.

Cassie wasn't the only one who thought so. Whenever they came across a female Marine, Cassie noticed the appreciative looks they gave him. To give him credit, Sam didn't appear to say or to do anything to encourage their attention. But he garnered it all the same.

Cassie stood aside and observed his interaction as he chatted with a group of Marines. They'd reached the hangars where Marine Helicopter Squadron One was located. Cassie already knew that one of the squadron's missions was transporting the President. Banners hung proclaiming the squadron was the "First and Finest."

Spotting a young woman Marine nearby, Cassie stopped her and explained that she was a journalist doing a story on Sam. "I'd like to get a female's perspective," Cassie told the young woman, who said she was a mechanic. "Do you know Sam Wilder?"

"Everyone here knows Captain Wilder, ma'am. We admire him tremendously, ma'am." She seemed nervous about speaking to Cassie so she didn't press her further. But a while later, Cassie did overhear the young woman speaking to another woman in camouflage uniform.

"He's mighty fine. Has a heart of Teflon though. You know what they say, that no woman ever sticks very long to Captain Sam Wilder's heart."

"Don't let that reporter hear you say that or she'll put it in her story."

Cassie moved closer to Sam. He immediately pulled her into his circle, introducing her to everyone present. There was an unmistakable camaraderie especially among the pilots. She could read the hunger in Sam's eyes, his desire to return to flying. She doubted anyone else noticed, but she did.

Cassie knew how hard it must be to be held back from doing something you loved. She'd always loved to write. But her mother hadn't seen any purpose in her "scribblings" as she'd put it. She'd even burnt her journals once. "You need to go out and make money, Cass," her mom had told her. "I can't keep supporting you forever."

It didn't matter that Cassie had been the one making the little money left after her mother bought alcohol and cigarettes stretch to include food and shelter. It didn't matter that Cassie was the one who tried to smooth out a ruffled landlord's feathers when they were late paying the rent. It didn't matter that Cassie had been the responsible one. Her mother had never considered it to be enough, had never considered that Cassie had ever done enough.

No matter how much things change, they stay the same. That's what her mother used to tell her. And despite the fact that Cassie had traveled so far from those hungry years, despite the fact that she'd changed her appearance, inside she remained the same. The little girl looking in from the outside, watching as other people celebrated Thanksgiving and Christmas, and telling herself that she didn't care, that someday she'd live her dream. She'd be a writer.

Remember that, Cassie wrote in her notebook. *You're a writer. Don't ever forget it.*

Pasting a confident smile on her face, she joined the conversation. "So, fellas, tell me what Sam Wilder is *really* like."

"They don't have anything as tasty as Crying Tiger on the menu here for lunch," Sam said as he held open the door for her.

They'd moved on from the hangar to the commissary. "No? So chicken à la king is as exotic as they get here?"

"Just about."

He picked up a tray and handed it to her before taking one for himself. She'd noticed that his manners were impeccable that way. Now that she thought about it, he'd held out the chair for her last night at the restaurant, as well. And always opened doors for her.

She wasn't used to anyone opening doors for her. She'd always managed on her own. It felt a little strange to have someone doing these things for her.

Don't get used to it, she warned herself. This story will be over soon and you'll never see Sam again. You'll be back to opening your own doors soon enough.

That realization left her feeling a bit hollow inside. Which worried her big-time. Because it meant that she was getting too attached to the subject of her story.

In the beginning Cassie had been confident that she could keep her journalistic distance from Sam, but the more time she spent with him, the more she found that he was far more dangerous to her peace of mind than she'd anticipated. Sam was definitely more than just the cocky flyboy she'd expected.

She had to do something to keep him at bay. As she went through the line, ordering a salad and a diet soda, she mentally went over ways of doing that. She didn't even notice that Sam had added a big slice of carrot cake to her tray until they arrived at a table.

He shrugged and gave her one of his potent grins. "You looked hungry to me."

Wrong thing to say.

Cassie froze at the flashback. Pitying eyes of one cafeteria lady watching Cassie as she stood indecisively at the end of the line in the school cafeteria, counting the small change to see if she had enough to buy a single hot dog today. "You look hungry to me. Here, take some macaroni and cheese and you just tell the cashier that Marge gave it to you no charge."

Cassie had been so hungry she'd taken the handout that day. But she couldn't do it again, because then people would start asking questions about why she was hungry and the authorities would get involved. Her mother had warned her about talking too much. *"They'll put you in a juvenile hall with a bunch of delinquents. You think you've got it bad now, it's nothing compared to what goes on in those places."*

"Hey, are you okay?"

It took her a second or two to realize the question had come from Sam and not from the haunting memories of her past.

"If you don't want the cake, no problem. I'll eat it." He reached across the table to remove the offending dessert.

Cassie refused to give in to her past. "Touch that cake and you die," she warned with her customary feistiness.

He smiled as if relieved at her reaction.

"If you want dessert, there are plenty of bowls of Jell-O up there just waiting for you."

"I'm not a Jell-O guy."

He was doing it again, getting to her, endearing himself to her. She had to put a stop to it.

"No, you're a guy used to taking the easy way out."

Now he was the one who froze. "Excuse me?"

"It must be nice to have your life all laid out for you. No need to make decisions on your own, no need to make sacrifices. It was easy for you to follow in your family's footsteps by becoming a Marine. A real no-brainer. I suspect a lot of things have come easily for you, Sam."

Angry as he was, Sam had to silently admit there

was an element of truth in her words. Things *had* always come easy for him—women, the Marine Corps, flying. As the youngest in the family, he'd often silently taunted himself with the fact that there was nothing he could do that his brothers hadn't already done. Including being a hero. His oldest brother Justice had saved a child's life while off duty. Sam had just been doing his job when he'd landed that plane safely.

Since that fateful day, Sam had wondered what it was he really wanted out of life. Was Cassie right? Had he only chosen the Marine Corps because it was the easy thing to do?

Outwardly, Sam didn't allow his self-doubts to show. "I didn't realize you were a psychologist as well as a journalist."

She appeared surprised by his calm reply. "You're not going to contradict me? Tell me I don't know what I'm talking about?"

So she'd been looking for a fight. Interesting. Why would she do that? No reason he could think of, unless she was trying to gain some distance between them.

There was definitely more to Cassie than met the eye. He'd seen the way she'd reacted when he'd said she'd looked hungry. While many women suffered from eating disorders, he didn't think that was the case with her. She had a great body, curved in all the right places. Lusciously curved.

No, it was almost as if she'd gone somewhere in her past when he'd mentioned going hungry. Did it have something to do with her childhood?

He knew firsthand that your upbringing molded you into the person you became. Sure, there were other factors along the way. But childhood provided the foundation. He knew nothing about her background while she knew a great deal about his.

She had a way of making him look at things differently. She was certainly making him look at *her* differently. There was so much more to her than just a pretty face. She made him think, made him dig deeper with her challenges.

"Tell you that you don't know what you're talking about?" he said, picking up on her previous comment. "I'd never dream of doing such a thing, ma'am."

"Oh, get over this ma'am stuff would you please?"

"It's meant as a sign of respect."

"I don't want to say sir to you every time we speak, so let's just return to using first names, okay?"

"Understood."

That was clearly another military thing—using words such as "affirmative" and "understood." She wondered why he hadn't gotten angry when she'd accused him of taking the easy way out. Instead he was studying her as if she were a coded message he was trying to decipher. Which wasn't her intention at all. She didn't want him paying more attention to her.

So her big plan backfired.

"It occurs to me that you know a lot about my background yet I know very little about yours."

Uh-oh. Definitely not a good sign. "That's because I'm interviewing you, not the other way around."

"And if I were interviewing you, what would you tell me?"

"Nothing at all."

He nodded. "I figured as much. You asked about my family. We're close. We're competitive. We're Marines. Enough said."

* * *

"I thought you liked taking risks," Sam said a few hours later.

"That doesn't mean I'm stupid enough to climb into a fighter jet with you."

"You don't trust me?"

"No further than I can toss you, buddy. I've heard about civilians taking rides in fighter jets and ending up using barf bags. No thank you. That's an experience I can do without."

"It would give you something to write about."

"You can just turn off the charming smile, it's not going to work. I'm staying here on terra firma. Which reminds me, I need to make a phone call and my cell phone battery is dead. Can I use the phone in the office over there?"

Sam nodded and watched in admiration as she walked away. She had the sexiest sashay. A sudden thump on his back distracted him.

"Looks like you lost that round. Score one for the feisty girl reporter."

"Don't let her hear you call her that, Striker," Sam warned his buddy.

Actually, Striker was Sam's oldest brother Justice's good buddy. Both men had met in Force Recon Marines. Justice had suffered injuries in an accident that had removed him from active duty. He was now teaching prospective recruits for the elite special forces.

Striker was still in Force Recon. He had dark hair and green eyes, but the most striking thing about him was his intensely guarded demeanor. Unless he was dealing with a fellow Marine.

"I hear you did the Corps proud with your smooth landing," Striker said.

"It wasn't all that smooth," Sam said.

"Smooth enough."

"I didn't know you were here at Quantico."

"Not for long." Much of what Striker did was classified and divulged only on a need-to-know basis. Sam had learned not to ask for details. "But let's get back to you and the girl reporter. What's the deal there?" Striker asked.

"She's doing a story on me for some magazine. She's following me around for a week or two, to get a feel what it's like to be a Marine."

Striker grinned and eyed her retreating figure with blatant male appreciation. "She can get a feel for this Marine anytime."

"Watch it, Striker. Hands off," Sam growled.

"'Hands off'?" Striker repeated with a raised brow.

"She's special," Sam said.

"She must be to make you look like that," Striker replied.

"Like what?"

Striker laughed. "Give it up, buddy. I know a lovestruck leatherneck when I see one."

"I only met the woman yesterday."

"So? She works fast."

"She's working, period. As a journalist. Writing this story on me."

Striker nodded mockingly. "You keep telling yourself that."

"It's just that we're stuck with each other for the next week or two—"

"Stuck together?" Striker interrupted him. "Doesn't that raise any red flags with you?"

"What are you talking about?"

"That all your brothers married the women they were 'stuck' with. Think about it. Joe and Prudence were stuck in a snowbound cabin. Mark was stuck baby-sitting Princess Vanessa in New York City. And most recently, Justice and Kelly were stuck together in my beach house. This is too rich. History repeating itself as the last Wilder bachelor has finally met his match!" He delivered this last sentence like a sportscaster calling the World Series.

"You're certifiable, Striker, you know that?"

"Me? You're the one falling for a woman you only met yesterday. This from the guy rumored to have a Teflon heart."

Sam grimaced. "Yeah, that's certainly what I've worked for all my life, to be compared to nonstick cookware. Just the thing any Marine strives for."

"Hey, you were the one who declared at Justice's wedding a few months ago that you were planning on making the most of being the last Wilder bachelor."

"That's still the plan."

"Then you better revise that plan, because that dog's just not gonna hunt, as my Texas grandaddy would say."

"Your oilman millionaire Texas grandaddy?"

"Yep, that's the one. On my momma's side of the family."

"He still disowning you and your brothers because you joined the Marine Corps?"

"Affirmative. He never did forgive my momma for marrying a Kozlowski from Chicago, and a Marine to boot. Us boys joining up only made things worse in his eyes. Millionaire oilmen don't have grandsons in the Marines. You're lucky you come from a family of leathernecks.''

"Yeah, lucky.'' It didn't feel that way all the time, though. Sometimes it felt as if he'd taken the easy way, just like Cassie had said. Everyone in his family expected him to become a Marine, so as the youngest of four sons, he'd done what was expected. "Following in my brothers' footsteps isn't always a piece of cake. No pleasure cruise.''

"Good thing that Marines never go on pleasure cruises. We go where others fear to tread. *Semper fi!*''

"*Semper fi!*'' Sam high-fived him.

"Did I miss something?'' Cassie asked as she rejoined them.

"No, ma'am,'' Sam quickly replied.

"Who's your friend?'' she asked Sam with a nod toward the Marine at his side.

"Striker Kozlowski at your service, ma'am.'' He took her hand in his, holding it longer than Sam thought was appropriate.

For once Cassie wasn't paying attention to the expression on Sam's face. Instead she was focusing on Striker. In his own way, he was as good-looking as Sam and the look in his green eyes clearly sent the message that he found her attractive. But he also gave her the impression of a man who disguised himself and his true emotions well.

"So, Striker, are you a pilot like Sam?''

"No, ma'am.''

He didn't elaborate beyond those two words.

"So you're the tall, dark and silent type, is that it?'' she teased him.

"He's the type you shouldn't mess with,'' Sam

stated in a tone of voice she'd never heard before. It wasn't anger or even bossiness. It was something else, some other emotion...

Was Sam jealous? Surely not. Cassie found the possibility almost unbelievable. Sam was an incredibly confident man, sure of his sex appeal where members of the opposite sex were concerned.

Sure, Striker was no slouch in the looks department, but he represented a darker side that Cassie had no desire to explore. Which surprisingly enough, made her feel more comfortable with Striker than she did with Sam. It felt safer teasing Striker, even flirting with him a little, because she was in no danger with Striker. No danger at all of losing her head, or her heart.

She could no longer say the same about Sam.

Chapter Four

Cassie loved her bed, loved the soft white duvet and the sensual deep-ruby chenille pillows. It was her haven. It was her safe place.

The problem was that a true Tough Chick should not need a safe place. A Tough Chick didn't need a romantic bedroom with dreamy white drapes framing a whimsical curlicue-iron bedstead.

But then Cassie's toughness was only surface deep. Which was why this Tough Chick had the covers over her head despite the fact that it was five in the afternoon and Sam would be picking her up in less than two hours from now.

The bottom line was that she dreaded going to this stupid black-tie event tonight.

It would be her first outing in a formal dress as a whiplash blonde. She tried whipping up enthusiasm by reminding herself of that fact, but only got a lukewarm reception from her stern inner critic.

Who do you think you're kidding with this make-over routine? You're not fooling anyone.

Cassie tried telling herself she was a bit shaky from that flashback moment in the commissary earlier. She tried telling herself that she was just tired from too little sleep.

Then she gave herself another five minutes to play possum under the covers before getting ready. Meditation was good for the soul. Hiding under the covers was her form of meditation, her way of wiping out the hectic world, of erasing things that upset her—such as her attraction to Sam, the sexy Marine with the Teflon heart.

His buddy Striker had also been good-looking, but he hadn't struck a receptive nerve within her the way Sam had. Why not? What was it about Sam that got to her? His blue eyes? She'd seen guys with blue eyes before. His muscular build? The firefighter she'd interviewed had been just as muscular, but he hadn't done a thing for her sexually.

She needed to figure out what the deal was with her attraction to Sam so that she could fight it and deal with it. Because there was no way she was falling for him. That would be an incredibly stupid thing to do. He wasn't what she was looking for. In fact, she wasn't even looking for a man in her life right now. She was focusing on her career, on her writing.

That's how she had to think of this evening. As an extension of her work. She just needed to pretend she was a fly on the wall, taking notes of what everyone else was doing, of Sam's reaction to the ritzy crowd. And she had no doubt the crowd would be ritzy, with very deep pockets. Sam's duty was to be on show as the Marine poster boy. Her duty was to record it all in her notes. It really didn't matter what she wore.

Yeah, right.

Okay, so she had one conservative black tuxedo-type pantsuit she wore for evening events. She really should wear that. It's what she'd always worn on the few occasions she'd had to attend one of these things in the past....

But she was a whiplash blonde now, one who could finally carry off that strapless little burgundy number hanging in the back of her closet like a guilty secret.

She'd bought it on sale a few days after getting her hair colored. She had yet to muster the guts to actually wear it. Not that the dress was unduly sexy or revealing. No, the beauty of it was in the cut and the way it fit Cassie, hugging her body with perfection.

Cassie would need all the confidence she could muster to get through this evening. Hanging around with a bunch of people who had more money than they knew what to do with never failed to push her insecurity buttons, making her feel like the outcast she'd been as a child. So she should wear the dress and play the role of whiplash-blond Tough Chick for all it was worth.

Having finally made that decision, Cassie tossed the covers off and leapt out of bed. Half an hour later she'd showered and dressed. Then she'd completed a makeup routine laid out by the technician who'd worked with Ivan at the salon. Cassie had come home with a bag of new cosmetics and a step-by-step diagram of what went where for daytime or nighttime looks. She had to put her contacts in first to see what she was doing.

By the time she was done she almost didn't recognize herself for a moment. The body-skimming, full-length sheath needed no further adornment so she'd tied a simple but elegant black silk ribbon around her neck with the ends dangling tantalizingly close to her cleavage.

The sparkling studs in her ears and the ring on her right finger weren't real diamonds, but were a believable size.

Now for shoes. Her running shoes wouldn't do. Neither would her black chunky loafers or her suede clogs. This dress needed killer shoes, so called because they often killed the woman wearing them. At least that had always been Cassie's view in the past. But when she'd bought the dress, the saleslady had insisted Cassie buy shoes to go with it.

She slipped on the barely-there high-heeled shoes, added a dash of exotic perfume—and presto!—insecure Cassie was transformed into powerhouse Cassandra.

She left her bedroom and headed for the living room, making sure everything was in order there. The apartment had an unusual floor plan, but then the entire building had a character all its own. Built in the 1920s, it celebrated craftsmanship—from the multipaned arched windows in the main floor lobby to the Gothic-inspired light fixtures in every apartment's dining room. It didn't celebrate practicality necessarily but she loved the place anyway.

From her bedroom, Cassie turned left into the large living room. If she'd gone straight on down the hall she would have entered her dining room and from there her kitchen. If she'd turned right she would have been in the tiny bathroom.

The main focus in her living room was the cranberry-red sectional couch placed in the corner near the French doors leading out to a small wrought-iron balcony. A fringed jute rug picked up the neutral color of the walls while the cheerful striped pillows picked up the red from the couch. Her TV and DVD were hidden away in a compact wooden armoire that she'd picked up at the flea market near historic Capitol Hill. Simply framed black-and-white photos of Washington, D.C., landmarks, some taken by Al, were placed around the room. A solid pine bench in a distressed-red barn finish served as a coffee table and held a colorful Jamaican ceramic bowl, another find from the flea market.

Cassie loved the bold splash of color provided by the couch and the large acrylic painting of a single red poppy that took up most of one wall. She didn't have a lot of things, but what she did have, she loved.

She checked her appearance in a mirror propped on the white console table in the postage-stamp entryway by the front door. The white-distressed finish gave both the mirror and the table a vintage farmhouse look. Her look, on the other hand, was anything but vintage. It was classy.

Okay, she could do this. She was a whiplash blonde on a mission. She was ready for anything.

Except Captain Sam Wilder in a U.S. Marine dress blues uniform.

She was struck again by how impossibly attractive he was. His dark hair lay smoothly against his head while the dark fringe of his lashes surrounded those awesome dark blue eyes of his. But it was more than just Sam's looks, it was the sheer physical impact of him—the way he held himself with military erectness, the way he epitomized power and strength.

"Wow." Sam didn't say another word, but then he didn't have to. His eyes were more expressive than any husky compliment could have been.

"I could say the same about you. Wow," she murmured in return.

"Thank you, ma'am. It's the dress blues uniform. Best uniform of any branch of the armed services."

"There's that Marine Corps confidence again."

"I prefer to think of it as esprit de corps."

She preferred talking about the Marine Corps in general rather than focusing on one sexy Marine in particular. It gave her a chance to catch her breath.

That didn't last long once they entered the small confines of the gilded elevator. Sam had gallantly placed his hand on the small of her back as he guided her inside. A ripple of anticipation shivered up her spine. The most polite of touches, yet her response was undeniably sensual.

The scrollwork doors were about to close when someone cried, "Hold the elevator!"

Sam, being the gentleman he was, pushed the open-door button.

Cassie recognized the woman's voice. Mrs. Friedman was the building's most avid gossip. Her husband was no doubt at her side, although the man never said much. The poor guy probably couldn't get a word in edgewise.

"My, but you look lovely this evening, Cassandra. Doesn't she, Saul?"

Saul nodded, the bald spot on the top of his head shining in the overhead light of the elevator.

Looking at Sam, the older woman said, "I don't believe we've met. I'm Rebecca Friedman and this is my husband Saul." The words *And you are?* may have remained unspoken but they were very clear nonetheless.

"It's nice to meet you, ma'am. Captain Sam Wilder, U.S. Marines, at your service."

"Oh, my." Mrs. Friedman touched her wrinkled hand to her bosom as Sam flashed her a smile. "I didn't realize you were dating a man in uniform, Cassandra."

"We're not dating," Cassie hurriedly corrected her. She certainly didn't want any rumors getting started. "I'm writing a story about Captain Wilder."

"A story about dating a Marine? How romantic."

"No," Cassie corrected her again. "A story about American heroes."

"So you're dating an American hero? Even more romantic. My Saul here could have been a hero, but a childhood illness left him a tad deaf in one ear so he couldn't join the military." She patted her husband's arm fondly. "But he's still a hero in my book. We'll be celebrating our forty-fifth wedding anniversary in December."

"Congratulations to you both," Sam said.

"Yes, congratulations," Cassie said, willing the elevator to move faster. Like the rest of her building, it dated back to the 1920s when elegance was more important than efficiency or speed.

"We've been meaning to thank you, Cassandra dear, for helping us finally get those fraudulent phone charges off our bill." Turning to Sam, she added, "We wrote dozens of letters and made numerous phone calls, but nothing was done until Cassandra here stepped in."

Cassie shrugged, uncomfortable with this kind of attention. "It wasn't me, it was the power of the mighty pen. I did a story about telemarketers adding bogus phone charges and used the Friedmans' case as an example,'' she told Sam.

The elevator finally shuddered to a stop. There was a pause before the doors slowly opened. Cassie would have leapt out of the elevator like a shot were it not for the fact that Sam had his hand cupped around her elbow and the fact that her killer shoes prevented her from making any sudden moves.

"Enjoy your evening," Mrs. Friedman said with a wave. "Saul and I are going to our favorite restaurant for dinner. Maybe you two can join us sometime."

Cassie just nodded and smiled vaguely while returning the older woman's wave.

"Nice lady," Sam noted as he led Cassie to his car parked just down the street.

The evening air held the warmth of an Indian summer with just a hint of autumn chill yet to come.

"How did you find a parking space so close?" The ten-block Woodley Park area was known for its neat yards in front of quaint old houses and for its row houses amid large trees and lovely gardens. It was infamous, however, for its lack of parking along its tree-lined streets.

Holding the car door open, Sam gave her a quizzical look. "Someone was pulling out as I came by."

"Oh, so you're one of those," she noted.

"Those?"

"The lucky kind."

"I can only hope," he murmured with a heated look that traveled from her head to her toes.

"That's not what I meant," she muttered, feeling a blush heat her cheeks. Cassandra Jones, Tough Chick Journalist, should not be blushing.

Gathering her composure and the fringed black silk scarf she was using as a shawl, Cassie slid into his low-slung car.

"Nice wheels," she said with an appreciative look at the sports car's high-tech dash.

"It's a rental. I'm out of the country too much to have a car of my own."

Sam's words reminded her yet again about the impermanence of his lifestyle. She certainly knew how that went. Cassie had moved around often with her mother, always one step ahead of an angry landlord or bill collector.

"Why did it make you feel uncomfortable having your neighbor say nice things about you?"

Cassie blinked in surprise at his question. "What makes you think I was uncomfortable?"

"Your body language."

"You're imagining things."

"I certainly have imagined a few things where you're concerned, and seeing you in that lovely dress tonight is making me imagine a few more, but I didn't imagine your reaction to her comments. What was wrong? Did you think it would tarnish your Tough Chick image for me to know that you'd done a good deed for your elderly neighbors?"

"I told you, I was just doing my job."

He smiled. "Now that's a sentiment I can relate to."

His hand lowered to the gearshift located on the floor between their seats. Checking the mirror first, he smoothly drove the car away from the curb. His driving style was all about controlled power, not showy but confident.

Cassie watched his hand gripping the rounded shift

and imagined his hands controlling the power of a plane, or the power of a woman. He had long, lean fingers, surprisingly artistic-looking for a warrior. And that's what he was. Despite the polish, he was a warrior, trained to preserve and protect America's freedom. Her freedom.

She should be grateful to him and all the men and women like him. The trouble was, there wasn't anyone quite like Sam. There certainly never had been in her life. No one who got to her the way he did. No one who threatened her peace of mind the way he did. No, Captain Sam Wilder was definitely one of a kind.

"Can we leave yet?" Cassie asked.

"We just got here."

"I know." She sighed. "I was just kidding."

But Sam had his doubts. She'd been acting strangely since he'd picked her up. For one thing she'd been unusually quiet in the car. That wasn't like her at all.

And then there had been that scene with her neighbors in the elevator. Despite what Cassie said, he'd had the distinct impression that she'd felt extremely awkward about their comments. He couldn't help wondering if she was trying to protect her Tough Chick image.

Looking at her now, wearing that awesome gown, Sam thought she was the most stunning woman in the room. And he wasn't the only one. He could practically hear the jaws drop as he walked into the ballroom with her.

Yet he could have sworn he felt her fingers tremble slightly as they rested on his arm.

"Not nervous, are you?" he deliberately challenged her.

As he'd hoped, she raised her chin and gave him a confident look. "Of course not."

"Good, because you've got nothing to be nervous about. You're Cassandra Jones, talented *Capital Magazine* reporter, and all-around Tough Chick."

"These aren't exactly Tough Chick stomping grounds," she noted wryly.

"No?"

"No. These are Rich Chick stomping grounds. Princesses born with a silver spoon in their mouths, family pedigrees that go back to the *Mayflower*. I feel like Cinderella at the ball," she said kiddingly.

"Yeah, right. I can see you waiting for some prince to figure out your shoes size before coming to get you. You're too proactive for that. You're not the type to wait around for someone else."

"What type am I?"

"The type that can make a guy like me believe in fairy tales."

"I thought you said I wasn't the fairy-tale type."

"I said you weren't the Cinderella type. There's a difference."

She couldn't comment further because they'd arrived at their table. Sure enough, it was already filled with just the sort of people Cassie had been afraid of meeting. The women sized her up in a quick look, tallying up the cost of her gown and finding it wanting compared to their own high-priced designer duds.

Cassie returned their stares, deliberately refusing to turn away. She hoped her look said *So who's the smarter woman here, the one who paid thousands for a dress she'll only wear once or the one who walks in with the sexy Marine on her arm?* She hoped her look didn't say *I don't belong here.*

Sam, ever the gentleman, held out her chair for her and made a point of paying her a great deal of attention as she settled in her seat.

Cassie appreciated his efforts to make her feel comfortable and tried to distract herself by taking note of her surroundings. The event was being held at the Willard, one of Washington's most prestigious old hotels, dating back to before the turn of the century. Since this was a U.S.O. fund-raiser, they'd gone with patriotic themes throughout. Tiny red, white and blue lights gleamed from white pillars set around the outer walls. Table decorations included miniature American flags and sparkling red and blue stars.

Dinner was surprisingly good. She particularly liked the endive, watercress and beet salad with walnut dressing. She only knew those details because it was written on a tiny menu placed beside the silverware. As the meal progressed, she was content to let the conversation flow around her. After all, she was here as an observer.

And she observed plenty. Such as the way the women at their table all flirted with Sam. Some were more discreet than others, but they all had a touch of simpering in their attitude that Cassie prayed she never displayed.

Leaning over to Sam in between courses, she said, "If I ever start batting my eyelashes at you like that, just shoot me and put me out of my misery."

He laughed.

"I'm serious," she said in a solemn whisper.

"Somehow I don't think that will ever be a problem."

"I certainly hope not. Now are you going to eat that cinnamon chocolate brownie or would you like me to finish it for you?"

"It's all yours."

"The raspberries and blueberries in the dollop of whipped cream make this a patriotic dessert."

"Healthy, too, with fresh fruit."

"Chocolate is always healthy," Cassie replied, closing her eyes a moment to enjoy the delectable taste. "Mmm, especially *good* chocolate."

Sam watched the way her tongue slipped around the outside of her mouth to catch every last crumb. He shifted in his seat, getting aroused just by watching her eat a brownie. She was wearing a sexy wet lipstick that matched her dress and didn't seem to disappear no matter how many times she delicately licked her lips.

He groaned, dying to taste her for himself, to test the staying power of her lipstick by trying to kiss it off her while taking that awesome dress off at the same time.

"Let's dance," he practically growled.

He had her up and out of her seat before she knew what happened. "I'm no good at dancing," she said even as he led her to the dance floor.

"Just follow my lead."

"You already know I'm not good at following," she reminded him.

"Only one of us can lead while we're dancing."

"Which is why we shouldn't dance."

"Come on, you can do it." He took her slender hand in his much larger one while splaying a warm palm against her back. "It's not that difficult."

But it was difficult, in the most delicious of ways.

She was infinitely aware of each and every place where he touched her. Her hand was clasped in his, his fingers intertwining with hers. His body brushed against hers as he swept her up into a gentle waltz. He guided her with utter confidence, holding her in his arms as if she were someone precious.

They were in the middle of a crowded dance floor, surrounded by people, yet she felt caught up in the unexpected magic of a circle of intimacy flowing between Sam and her. The sensitized tips of her fingers brushed against the smooth material of his uniform.

He was holding her close, but no closer than any of the other couples around them. Yet the hidden sexual radiance of his embrace warmed her to the core. There was something forbidden here, something unknown, something incredibly powerful.

Everything else was forgotten in that moment of intense connection. The rest of the world was shut out, along with her fears and her vows of objectivity. The only thing left was Sam, holding her, sliding his fingers through hers and creating an erotic friction that filled her with a blind yearning.

Cassie didn't realize the music had stopped until Sam reluctantly came to a halt. Even then, he kept her in his arms and close to his heart.

Until someone interrupted them a second later.

"Can I have the next dance?" Striker asked Cassandra.

His appearance brought her back down to earth as she nervously stepped away from Sam.

"What are you doing here, Striker?" Sam asked, clearly surprised at seeing him.

"Enjoying dancing with a beautiful woman," Striker replied as he swept Cassie away.

Like Sam, Striker looked handsome in his dress blues uniform. But unlike Sam, he didn't make her heart beat the least bit faster.

"Take pity on my buddy over there," Striker said. "Don't go giving him too hard a time, okay? That's my job."

His words surprised her. "Are you afraid I'm going to write something negative about him?"

"Marines aren't afraid, ma'am."

"Sam told me that they overcome fear."

Striker sighed. "He always was one for honesty."

Cassie winced inwardly. She didn't feel very honest in showing Sam this fancy facade when she didn't have the inner chutzpah to totally back it up. Rebecca and Saul Friedman wouldn't approve. After forty-five years of marriage they no doubt were totally honest with one another.

Cassie couldn't imagine how that would feel. Revealing yourself to someone else so completely it left you vulnerable, too vulnerable. She just couldn't see herself doing that only to have the person she loved walk away, leaving her alone.

"You don't have to worry about Sam," she stated firmly. "Ours is merely a working relationship. I'm writing a story about him. Nothing else."

"Right." Striker's voice was clearly mocking. "That's what he tells me, too."

"Then you should listen to us both."

"And mind my own business, right?" Striker added.

She nodded firmly.

"Okay, fair enough. It's not like I'm any expert in the love department." He laughed a tad bitterly.

"Give me something simple, like covert tactical maneuvers, any day. Love can be the pits."

"Amen," she said.

"You're different, though. You might be good for Sam. He's never had to actually chase after a woman before. They usually chase after him. Runs in his family. But they all eventually met women who met their match. All except Sam. Until now. Yeah, I think you might be good for Sam."

Shaken by his words, Cassie excused herself the moment the music ended and hastily made her way to the ladies' room, looking for a moment's peace and quiet so that she could regain her composure.

But she'd no sooner walked into the ladies' room than she was confronted by *Capital Magazine*'s society writer, Sonya Heyden. The woman gave divas a bad name. Suspected to be in her early fifties although no one knew for sure, she had short black hair, narrow brown eyes, and skinny lips. She also had a big mouth. Half the people at the magazine were afraid of her, the other half just avoided her. Cassie would have done that, but it was too late. Sonya had spotted her already.

"I must say, I was surprised to see you here." The older woman's voice was condescending.

"I'm doing the story on Captain Wilder for the 'Week in the Life of an American Hero' series."

"Oh, right." She capped her expensive lipstick before staring at Cassie in the mirror. "How...quaint that you got that story after changing your appearance. I guess what they say about blondes having more fun is true after all."

"Just what are you insinuating?"

"Why nothing, dear. Some at the magazine might

have found it a little suspicious that an inexperienced young thing like you got this plum assignment.''

Cassie told herself she should turn the other cheek and walk away. But she couldn't. There was no way she wasn't going to defend her professional reputation. "I got this assignment because of my writing, not my looks."

"Sure you did." Sonya's voice was mocking. "I'm not saying I blame you. Quite the opposite. I think it was a clever move, changing your appearance the way you did and making Phil take notice."

"Phil wouldn't care what I looked like if I couldn't write."

"I never said you couldn't write. You are a capable writer. Nothing special, but competent. I'm merely pointing out that there are a number of other writers more qualified to write this article than you."

"You mean, someone like yourself," Cassie replied as the real reason for Sonya's hostility suddenly clicked into place.

"It's a human interest story. I certainly have years more experience covering this town."

"You're the society reporter. This isn't a society piece."

"Don't tell me what kind of piece it is," Sonya snapped. "I could have written it, but Phil wouldn't give me the chance."

Cassie had read Sonya's work and she knew why Phil had made that decision. She was a long-winded flowery writer enamored with her own brilliance. She lacked insight.

"Phil is a smart man," Cassie said. "I trust his judgment. And so should you. I don't care if you insult me, but by insinuating he only gave me this job because I'm a blonde now, you're demeaning him. The quality of my work is still the bottom line as far as Phil is concerned.'' She felt confident about that fact, because he'd made no bones about telling her. Her newfound attitude had made him think she was ready for this assignment, but it was her writing that mattered in the final analysis.

''So how does it feel knowing that everyone at the office is talking about you, speculating about the relationship between you and Phil?''

''Everyone I know at the office is too busy working and too smart to speculate about anything as bogus as Phil and I having anything but a working relationship.''

''So he sent you to seduce the soldier hero?''

''He's a Marine. They don't like being called soldiers. And I wasn't sent to seduce anyone.''

''I saw you and the Marine dancing together. You've certainly got him fooled. He should have seen you a few months ago. I bet he wouldn't have given you a second glance then.''

Sonya's words scored a direct hit on one of Cassie's most vulnerable areas.

Satisfied that she'd done her worst, the older woman walked out, leaving Cassie alone with her insecurities.

''Everything okay?'' Sam asked as he drove her home a short while later. ''You've been quiet ever since you danced with Striker. What's wrong? Did he say anything to you? Because if he did, all you have to do is tell me and I'll take care of him.''

His vehemence surprised her. ''I thought he was a friend of yours.''

"He's really more a friend of my oldest brother, Justice. I can't believe he upset you this way."

"Actually you sound more upset than I do. If I didn't know better, I'd say you almost sounded…jealous. But that would be ridiculous, right?"

"Absolutely. I don't have anything to be jealous about where Striker is concerned. I mean, it's not like you like the guy and want to go out with him or anything, right?"

"Right."

"Good. I'm glad we agree on that. Looks like I'm not going to get a parking space close to your building this time. Do you mind if we walk?"

"You can just drop me off in front of my building—"

"No, I can't."

"Yes, you can. I'd prefer it actually." That way she could hurriedly hop out of the car without dealing with any good-night kissing issues.

"Not necessary. There's a space up there."

She wouldn't have thought he could squeeze the car in, but he did, just barely. They only had to walk one block.

She had to admit it was a lovely evening for a stroll, still warm enough to be comfortable. A few colorful leaves crunched under their feet as they walked beneath the sheltering branches of a majestic old oak tree.

They'd almost reached her building when Cassie automatically paused to smell the flowers from the beautiful garden just on the other side of the black wrought-iron fence. Briefly closing her eyes, she drank in the heavenly smell of roses.

This was always a favorite stopping spot for her. Whenever she came home from a long day at work, the look and smell of this lovely garden always refreshed her soul and made her feel better about the rest of life.

"I've never met a Tough Chick who stops to smell the roses."

She turned to grin at him in the darkness. "Then it's about time you did."

"It's about time I did this…" Sam murmured, taking her into his arms and lowering his lips to hers.

Chapter Five

The kiss began as a gentle coupling of lips. His were warm and firm. The mood was one of a slow and subtle quest. That lasted all of about five seconds before everything flared out of control. Her hunger matched his as Sam kissed her with a passion that rendered her delightfully weak and provocatively powerful all at once.

He didn't make her feel like a virgin loner. He made her feel like a wild and wanton whiplash blonde, like a woman confident enough to reach for what she wanted, to respond to the best kiss she'd ever had, to kiss him back with equal pleasure and intensity.

This wasn't like her at all. Some distant part of Cassie's mind registered that fact even as she moved closer and parted her lips. Now the kiss took on an even more erotic feel that brought her to a new realm.

Heat pulsed through her entire body, spreading its

sensual warmth all the way down to her toes in those killer shoes.

She bent her knee and lifted one foot. Ah, that was even better. Somehow the movement had brought her body into even closer contact with his. She could feel the brass buttons of his uniform pressing against her. His lower torso was in close contact with hers, increasing the intimacy of their embrace even further.

Meanwhile the kiss continued with wild heat and unmitigated desire. His big hands cupped her face as he tilted her head back to deepen their kiss, his thumb brushing her cheek as his tongue stroked hers. He tasted and tested, discovering what brought her the most pleasure—tickling the roof of her mouth, seductively dipping into the warm depths in a way that drove her wild.

Her hands shifted from his shoulders to his face, where she cupped his face as he was cupping hers. She could feel the slight roughness of a hint of stubble against her fingertips, the ensuing friction creating its own zing of desire.

Oh, my, oh, my, oh, my. The breathless refrain danced through her mind as her arousal-drenched body craved *more, more, more.* It didn't matter that they were standing in the middle of the sidewalk, it didn't matter that anyone walking by could see them.

All that mattered was that he continue claiming her mouth as if it were the source of all his joy.

"Bad dog, come back here!" The shout only distantly registered in her dazed brain before she and Sam were almost toppled over by an exuberant Great Dane.

Nothing like a dog the size of a small pony to break off a kiss. She probably wouldn't even have noticed anything smaller, like a dachshund. No, it had taken something huge and slobbering to tear her mouth from Sam's. Or his from hers.

"I'm so sorry," a bespeckled banker-type apologized as he grabbed the Great Dane's collar and leash. "He got away from me."

Cassie could relate. That kiss had certainly gotten away from her. Galloped right out of control in no time at all.

"Bad dog," the man reprimanded the dog before apologizing again. "I'm so sorry he bothered you."

The Great Dane wasn't what had bothered Cassie, it had been Sam and the unexpectedly incredible way he kissed her.

Okay, sure, so she had wondered out of feminine curiosity what kissing him might be like. But she'd never anticipated that it would be like *that*.

Words escaped her, never a good sign for a writer. She tried to surreptitiously read Sam's expression, looking for a sign of gloating or triumph and instead finding a slightly dazed look in his blue eyes that she suspected matched the look in her own eyes.

Which meant what? That most women he kissed didn't kiss him back the way she had? Or that most kisses weren't like the one they'd just shared?

"I've got to go," she said, slipping away while Sam got caught up in the rambunctious Great Dane's leash.

Hurrying into her building she felt like Cinderella rushing from that ball at midnight, frantic to get away before her secret was discovered. She wasn't really a whiplash blonde at all. She was just Cassie, treading in dangerous waters with a man who had the power to make her want everything she couldn't have.

* * *

First thing on Saturday morning Cassie went to see her editor Phil because she'd spent a restless night tossing and turning over Sonya's words last night.

Okay, so if she was honest, the memory of Sam's kiss had also played a role in her restless night and was no doubt responsible for the hotly sexual dream that had woken her this morning and forced her to take a cold shower to cool down.

But she was at the magazine this morning because of Sonya. Not because she was avoiding Sam. No way. She'd had to come by to pick up her messages, check her mail, take care of business. She was a journalist. She couldn't just spend her days mooning after a sexy Marine. She had a job to do.

And there were a few things she had to clarify about the job. The weekend receptionist, Marilyn, waved as Cassie walked by and buzzed her into the magazine's headquarters. It was a fancy name for the large space occupied with cubbyholes, computers and monitors. Normally the place was filled with the sounds of people typing on keyboards blended with the whir of printers spitting out what they'd written. But it was relatively quiet on the weekends.

Phil had his own glassed-in corner office with a door he almost always kept open and blinds on the windows he almost always kept shut. Saturday mornings were his time to catch up. In his early fifties with a headful of gray hair, Phil possessed the keen intellect and people skills of a good manager. Photos of his wife and kids adorned his desk along with various baseball memorabilia and a cup filled with yellow pencils, one of which he was gnawing on as he answered her knock with his customary, "Enter."

Cassie had yet to figure out exactly how to raise the matter of why he'd selected her to write this series. She couldn't come right out and ask Phil why he'd given her this assignment, could she? No way. Partly because it wasn't a professional thing to do and partly because the imposter in her was afraid he'd say, "I have no idea why I gave you this story to do, I must have been crazy. It was a mistake. I really meant for someone else to do it."

Which was a wacky way to think. Cassie knew she was a good writer. She knew she deserved this chance. She just needed to hear it again from Phil. Luckily he gave her the perfect opening.

"So how's the article on the Marine going?" Phil asked.

"Pretty good so far."

"Good, glad to hear it. I just finished reading your piece on the firefighter. You did a great job with that. Remember when you kept hounding me to give you bigger assignments and I told you that your time would come?"

She nodded.

"Well, I was right. You needed time to grow into this job. There's something new in your writing that wasn't there before. Oh, don't get me wrong, you were always talented. But recently there's been something more. A deeper understanding, a newfound confidence. It's there in your choice of words, even in your sentence structure. I think that makeover thing you did was a good thing."

"But that's not why you gave me this assignment, right?"

"Because of your looks? No way. I gave you this series for the same reason I hired you in the first place.

Because you're a darn good writer. I have complete faith in your abilities. Now go out there and kick some Marine butt.'' At her startled look, he laughed and added, ''Just kidding. As a former Navy man myself, I was just indulging in a little interservice rivalry. But those days are long gone.'' He patted his middle-age tummy with wry acceptance. ''Now I'm just an editor who chews on pencils.''

Cassie knew the reason he did that. ''How long have you gone without a cigarette?''

''Seven weeks, two days and four hours, but who's counting?''

''Well, I for one am glad you quit smoking. We want you around for a long time to come.''

''That's the plan, kiddo. That's the plan.''

Cassie knew all about plans. She'd had a grand one where Sam was concerned. Too bad it wasn't working worth diddly-squat.

That was the problem with plans sometimes. They sounded real good when you were concocting them, but enacting them sometimes proved to be tricky.

It was Saturday. She'd be perfectly within her rights to say it was her day off and that she'd regroup with Sam on Monday. But the story was a week in the life, not the *work* week but the *entire* week, downtime, as well.

She knew what Sam would say. He'd say she was afraid. He'd say that he knew she couldn't keep up the schedule of staying by his side fourteen hours a day. He'd say she was avoiding him because of that kiss they'd shared last night. She could hear him now. The problem was she could often hear him; he had that kind of voice that stayed in a woman's mind.

Sam could turn a husky compliment into a priceless gift, then turn around and issue an order with the authority of a commanding officer. He could sound impressed and infuriated simultaneously. He could speak with confidence, he could tease with skill. And all of it was done in a deeply rich voice that made her savor the very sound of it.

Fine. She'd use the voice thing in her article somehow, without letting on that it pushed all her I-want-him buttons.

Sam never let her know ahead of time what was on the agenda for the day's activities. She suspected it was a powerplay, his way of keeping her off balance.

As if that would work. She'd played enough mind games with men, either in her professional life or her personal one, not to be bothered by them. Let him win this small skirmish while she went on to win the war.

The only thing he'd told her about his Saturday plans was that she wouldn't be interested in them. But Sam's very reluctance to talk to her about his schedule made her all the more curious about it. Which perhaps was his plan, but maybe not.

Either way, she'd pumped Striker a bit before leaving the ballroom last night and found out that Sam was working out with some underprivileged kids at a D.C. Boys and Girls Club today, playing some hoops.

Her intention was to slip into the facility undetected and to observe Sam interacting with the middle-school-age kids, both boys and girls. And at first she thought she'd succeeded in doing that, taking notes by hand so that the clicking of her laptop computer wouldn't give her away. She was seated way up in the bleachers near the door and had made sure to keep her entrance quiet.

But Sam was just biding his time. He was wearing the same black T-shirt with U.S.M.C. on it and the black running shorts that he'd worn that first morning they'd gone jogging.

Cassie momentarily got distracted watching him, noting the fact that he had the broad shoulders, flat stomach and narrow hips of a trained athlete. That's why she didn't see the basketball he tossed at her coming until it was almost in her face.

Her spiral notebook tumbled to the floor as she reflexively caught the ball.

"Nice save," Sam noted. "Why don't you come down here and help out while you're here. We're one short on the girls' team."

"How do you know I can even play basketball?"

"An educated guess."

"A lucky guess is more like it," she muttered even as she got up and headed down the bleachers to the gymnasium floor. While interning at a Chicago newspaper she'd participated in the impromptu games out in the parking lot, but she tended to play more by her instincts than by the rules.

"I believe this is yours." She tossed the basketball back to Sam with more force than was necessary. Of course he caught it with no difficulty at all.

"Nice move, Jones," Sam noted with a grin.

She sashayed closer, glad she'd elected to wear jeans and a red T-shirt. "To quote Julia Roberts, 'I've got moves you know nothing about'."

"Show me," he invited her. "Anytime, anyplace."

"In your dreams," she countered with a husky laugh.

"You most certainly are."

She wondered if he'd been kept up half the night remembering their kiss as she had. Then she reminded herself that she wasn't going to deal with that kiss today. "Okay, enough of this flirtatious banter, let's play ball."

An hour later the kids headed off to the showers while Sam wiped the sweat from his face and eyed Cassie with a newfound appreciation. "You're something else, you know that?"

"But of course," she said with airy humor. "You were expecting the boys to beat the girls team?"

"Not really, not when most of the girls are taller than the boys," he noted wryly.

"Girls mature earlier than boys. Of course, some would say that boys never mature at all, even when they're adults."

"No kidding? Some would say that? Like who? Like you for example?"

"On occasion, I've been known to say that, yes."

"But you wouldn't say that about me."

"I wasn't talking about you…necessarily."

"Necessarily." Sam pounced on that just as she'd known he would. "Which means?"

"That there are times when your competitive nature reminds me of kids vying for the same toy."

"Marines are competitive. We hate losing."

"Most people do."

"No, we *really* hate losing."

"Well, you lost today, buddy, and you managed to survive."

"What do you say we go get a pizza to celebrate?"

She checked her watch and was surprised to see that it was almost five. She'd skipped lunch, so she was hungry. "Sounds like a good idea. I need to get some more background information from you, about your family, that sort of thing. We can do that over pizza."

"You notice I haven't mentioned our kiss last night."

"You just did." Her heart gave a little kickbox in her chest. She'd been trying so hard to ignore that incredible kiss and for a while there she thought she'd done a darn good job of it, too.

"I figured you wouldn't be ready to talk about it just yet."

"You figured right," she said.

"So I figured I'd give you a little time."

"How generous of you."

He ignored the slight sarcasm in her voice. "So maybe after dinner tonight we can talk about it, or even better, do it again. Just to make sure that wasn't a one-time fluke."

"A fluke?" The man was saying that kissing her was a fluke? Maybe he'd been flying at high altitudes too long without enough oxygen. Okay, so she didn't have as much experience as he did, but still…a fluke?

"I can tell by the look on your face that I didn't put that right."

"No kidding."

"I meant that I wasn't expecting the kiss to be as…incredible as it was."

"I thought we weren't going to talk about the kiss."

"We aren't. I'm just putting the suggestion in your mind that we should consider doing it again, as a sort of experiment."

"I stopped experimenting with boys when I was

eight and they wanted to start playing doctor.'' Her voice was tart.

"I'm not a boy."

"I had noticed that," she replied. "You're something even worse. A Marine too darn sure of his own good looks and his charming ways with women. Well, I'm not about to be one of your experiments so you can just wipe that thought out of your mind."

"But I couldn't get you out of my mind. You have a way of making an unforgettable impression."

"We are not talking about that kiss and we are not repeating it. Understood?"

He just smiled. "You sounded a bit like a drill sergeant for a minute there."

"I'll take that as a compliment since it was the effect I was shooting for. Where should we go for pizza?"

"Mario's."

"Best Chicago-style deep dish in the D.C. area," she agreed.

Of course once they got to the restaurant in their separate cars, they argued over who arrived first in the parking lot. "There's that competitive nature coming out again," she warned him as he held the pizzeria door open for her.

"Takes one to know one," he retorted as he followed her inside.

Cassie paused a moment to inhale the divine scene of tangy tomato and Italian spices. They were shown to a booth in the back corner. Instead of sitting across from her, Sam scooted in beside her. "It gets pretty noisy in here on a Saturday night, and I might not be able to hear your questions sitting on the other side of the table."

"Likely story. You just want to sit closer so you can steal my slices of pizza easier. Think again, Captain."

"Oh, I'm thinking, all right," he murmured with a grin. "Don't you want to know what I'm thinking?"

"Absolutely not. I'd rather know what you want on your pizza."

Of course they then proceeded to argue over their selections and ended up with pretty much everything except for ham and pineapple on it.

The plan was to spend the rest of their meal talking about Sam's past. But as with so many of her plans where he was concerned, that didn't seem to happen. Instead they argued and discussed politics—he was more conservative than she was—and music and movies. Before she knew it, four hours had gone by and she still hadn't asked him her list of questions about his background.

Her lack of sleep was starting to catch up with her, that's why she had been so remiss in her interviewing techniques. She'd get an early night tonight and start fresh tomorrow.

"What's on the agenda for Sunday?"

"Not much. I thought I'd kick back and watch the football game on a big-screen TV at a local sports bar."

She was familiar with the place he named. "I'll meet you there."

And tomorrow, come what may, Cassie was sticking to her plan and to her interviewing questions. No more distractions.

The Grid Iron Sportsbar was a small place jam-packed with Washington Redskins fans. Tiny tables lined one wall while a bar lined the other. At the back was a large screen set high enough up that everyone could see it. Cassie arrived a few minutes before noon.

All the men turned to look at her as she entered the sports bar. It was an occurrence that only happened since she'd become a blonde. She'd also noticed that people tended to give her directions more slowly as if she'd be incapable of understanding them otherwise.

A beer commercial was playing on the TV while she scanned the room for Sam. Instead of waving her over to join him, he stood and came to meet her halfway. As always, he held out her chair for her.

The minute he returned to his own seat, she opened her laptop and began the questioning. "So tell me what it was like growing up as a Marine's kid."

"It was great."

"I need a little more to go on than that."

"We moved around a lot, got to see a lot of different places."

"Did that ever bother you? The frequent moving?"

"Not really. We always had each other."

"That must have been nice."

"I take it you don't come from a large family?"

"No." She quickly moved on to another question. "So tell me about competition between you and your brothers. Is that an issue with all of you in the Marine Corps?"

"Actually my brother Mark runs his own security business now. That was a fairy tale right there. Or a comedy of mishaps, if half of what my brother says is true. But I guess that's another story."

"Yes, it is." She remembered reading about Princess Vanessa of Volzemburg marrying a Marine Corps officer.

"Speaking of princesses," Sam continued, "I've been giving some more thought to which fairy tale suits you best, since you're not the Cinderella type."

"You clearly have too much free time on your hands," she replied.

Which was true. Sam was used to the high-adrenaline energy of flying missions every day. Sitting around at Quantico the past two and a half months was slowly driving him nuts. So was this sudden self-examination about his future in the Marine Corps. He'd never been one to question himself before, he'd always gone with the flow.

That emergency landing hadn't been his first brush with death but it had certainly been his closest. And he supposed it had changed him a little.

Okay, maybe it had even changed him a lot, he didn't know. Guys didn't wonder about internal stuff like that. And he wasn't altogether pleased that Cassie was making him think about it. But he was pleased to be able to spend time with her.

His attraction to her continued to grow with every passing moment. She was a never-ending surprise and a delicious challenge. Today she was wearing her Tough Chick T-shirt and jeans.

"I ordered the extra-spicy buffalo wings and the hot salsa and chips."

"I'll have some later. I want to get through these questions first. When did you first know you wanted to be a Marine?"

"Actually a Marine wasn't the first thing I wanted to be."

"It wasn't?"

He solemnly shook his head. "No."

"Then what was the first thing you wanted to be?"

"Batman. I liked his car."

She stifled a laugh. He'd set her up for that one with his serious voice and expression.

"So the Marine Corps came in a distant second to Batman, huh?"

"Not a distant second. What about you? I know you never dreamed of being Cinderella. How about Snow White? Can you see yourself as Snow White?"

"Hiding out with seven dwarfs, doing their housework? Not likely."

When he laughed, she realized how much she liked the sound. The sports bar was pretty noisy, but his laughter made a big impact on her. Not a good thing. Despite his determination to cast her as the heroine in some fairy tale, she wasn't the type.

She was a journalist who needed to keep her focus on the story. She decided that maybe questions weren't the best way to conduct this interview. "Talk to me about your family."

He started out slowly at first, watching the kickoff, dipping tortilla chips into the salsa. But he did talk and she did take notes, lots of them.

"My oldest brother Justice is the real hero in the family. He risked his life by saving a toddler from a burning car when he witnessed a car accident near Camp Lejeune in North Carolina. He suffered permanent injury to his shoulder as a result of that, which ended his ability to work as a Special Op Force Recon Marine."

"What's he doing now?"

"Enjoying his new wife and teaching Special Op forces the skills they'll need to survive."

"You were never tempted to go into Special Op work yourself?"

"No. I joined right out of high school and did some special computer training. It finally hit me that I wanted to fly, which meant I had to get a college education and get my commission as an officer. I was playing catch-up at that point. But it all worked out in the end, landing me here with you."

Sam realized that at that moment there was no place else he'd rather be. Which was strange for him. Usually he'd rather be in the cockpit of a plane than doing anything else. No woman had ever come close to his feelings about flying. But this woman was different.

For one thing, she was becoming increasingly caught up in the football game. "Are you a fan?"

"Sort of. When I was working at a small newspaper in northwestern Illinois, I covered everything from the zoning board meetings to the community theater group to the local kid who was playing special teams for the Bears. There were only two reporters so we pretty much did most of the work ourselves. Game day was a big thing in that town because of our local connection to the team. I guess I became a fan then."

She focused her attention back on the game. It was a low-scoring affair with defense playing the biggest role. Which was why her actions caught him by surprise. The Bears had made it into Washington Redskins' territory when Chicago's quarterback stepped back in the pocket, scrambling to find a receiver in the face of the defense's powerful pass rush.

The surrounding fans were shouting their approval until the quarterback miraculously escaped and somehow managed to throw the ball to a Bears' receiver in the end zone.

The place went silent as a tomb for a second, before Cassie leapt to her feet and shot both arms in the air. "Yeah, touchdown!" she shouted in excitement.

The Washington fans were not amused.

When it happened again ten minutes later, they were downright mad.

Sam had been in enough bars around the world to know when trouble was brewing. Thankfully the game was ending as he hustled her out of there, keeping her in front of him and shielding her with his body.

"You sure know how to make friends and influence people," Sam noted dryly.

She just grinned. "That's what we Tough Chicks do. Didn't you know that?"

He shook his head, only now realizing how much this particular self-proclaimed Tough Chick with her soft heart and her jungle-green eyes was coming to mean to him.

Chapter Six

Monday mornings Sam spent in the base's workout room, lifting weights instead of jogging on the track. He didn't realize he'd forgotten to share that bit of information with Cassie until she stormed into the room, headed straight for him with the precision of a guided missile.

She was wearing a red knit top and some kind of swirly, long skirt with little red flowers on it. A feminine outfit, nothing outrageous. Except that the top clung to her breasts and the skirt hugged her bottom. Every Marine in the place had their eyes glued on her as she made her way to him.

He'd never been a fan of long skirts, but he had to admit he liked the way this one fit her, showing off the swing of her hips as she walked. Sam had dated a model or two, and they had a thing about swinging their hips. But Cassie's movements were an integral part of her, like her wide luscious mouth.

It took Sam a second to realize he was still lying

on his back on the workout equipment, craning his neck to ogle her. He quickly sat up, almost knocking himself out with the crossbar of the weight above him.

Oh, yeah, he was definitely losing his edge. He was no desk jockey, he was an aviator. He didn't belong in the seat of a chair, he belonged in the cockpit of a plane. His frustration was mounting, and Cassie was to blame for that. Well, partially to blame.

If she hadn't been a reporter he could have told her about his feelings at being stuck in Quantico when he should be in action. But there was no way he could say that, not and risk it showing up in print. A good Marine never questioned his superior's mission statement. His assignment to Quantico was temporary and he could be called back into overseas duty at any time. He'd been told he'd return to flying soon.

Of course, flying would mean leaving Cassie behind. He wasn't ready for that yet.

Sam wasn't put off by Cassie's strength, or by her intelligence. He loved the way she gave as good as she got, loved her competitive nature. And he loved the way she looked as she stood in front of him, her hands on her hips, fire in her green eyes. "How long did you think you could hide out in here?" she demanded.

Her accusation ticked him off. "I wasn't hiding."

"I waited for you at the track for half an hour before I finally stopped someone and had them track you down."

"I'm sorry—" he began.

"If you were trying to avoid me it didn't work," she interrupted.

"I wasn't trying to avoid you. I just forgot to tell you."

"Likely story. You don't seem like the kind of man who forgets much."

"I don't," he growled irritably. "But you have a way of making me do things I don't normally do."

She certainly knew how that felt. Sam made her do things she didn't normally do, too. Such as stare at a man's physique. The black tank top Sam was wearing displayed the impressive play of muscles across his broad back as he turned to reach for a towel. The U.S.M.C. tattoo on his left arm actually rippled. "Let me just go shower and get dressed and we'll talk," he said.

Great, now she had the image of him standing naked beneath a shower, droplets of water running down his ruggedly handsome face, down his throat to gather at his collarbone before racing downward past his nipples and muscular chest to his navel and below.

"Yes…shower," she croaked. "I'll wait for you right outside. Outside the gym, I mean. Not outside the shower. Of course, I didn't mean outside the shower. I'm going now."

She didn't have to look back to know that he was grinning at her. She could feel it as she raced out of the gym.

By the time he rejoined her, she'd gathered her composure and her determination to get serious about this interview. They stopped at a coffee machine en route to his desk. Once there, she quickly got down to business. "Tell me why you love to fly."

"Are you familiar with the poem 'High Flight' by John Gillespie Magee Junior?"

Cassie shook her head.

"Well, that poem kind of expresses it best. He was an eighteen-year-old American who crossed the border into Canada to join the Royal Canadian Air Force before the U.S. was officially in World War Two. He was killed almost exactly three months after writing his poem when his Spitfire collided with a training plane." Sam's eyes held a newfound intensity as he recited the opening lines. "'Oh, I have slipped the surly bonds of earth and danced the skies on laughter-silvered wings.'" He paused a moment. "You should read the rest of it sometime."

Cassie had already made a note to look up the poem. Sam's deep voice had resonated with emotion when he'd spoken the World War Two poet's words. "It sounds magical."

"It is. There's nothing like the feeling of flying."

"When we visited the helicopter hangar the other day, I couldn't help noticing the hungry look in your eyes when the other Marines were talking about flying. You miss it, don't you?"

"Of course I do."

"Have you flown helicopters?"

"Affirmative. It requires special skills, because you don't use just your brain, you also have to coordinate your hands, feet, and eyes all together as if the controls were just an extension of your body."

"What would you prefer flying?"

"Whatever the Marine Corps needs me to fly."

"That's a diplomatic answer."

"It's the truth."

"What about the incident involving your crash landing? Have you flown since then?"

Sam nodded.

"Tell me about it."

"There's nothing to tell."

But the look in his eyes said otherwise. She

changed tactics. "Are you ever afraid of flying? Of dying?"

"All men feel fear, whether they admit it or not. It's something we study here, how to foster the courage to overcome fear in ourselves and in those we command."

"How do you do that?" Cassie had yet to overcome some of the deepest fears in her own life, instead keeping them deeply buried inside.

"It helps when you have strong leadership which earns the respect of subordinates. Leading by example. But everyone reacts differently. What may break the will of one man may only strengthen another's resolve to succeed. The Marine Corps uses training to instill that confidence to make sure that every Marine falls into the latter category, strengthening their resolve to win. Our basic training is longer than any of the other branches of the armed forces. Toughness is a combination of physical and mental resolve, which is why the Corps developed the Crucible as the culmination of basic combat training. Fifty-four gruelling hours with little food, little sleep, and a series of events that will test and tax them. Working as a team is crucial. In the end, the experience creates a change of mind, body, and spirit intended to last a lifetime."

"Does it last a lifetime?"

"In some Marines it does."

"It lasted in the Marines in your own family, didn't it?"

"Yes, even though my brother Mark left the Marine Corps to start his own security company."

"That's the brother who married the princess, right?"

"Right."

"Can you see yourself leaving the Marines the way he did?"

Sam shook his head firmly but inside he wasn't so sure. Mark was the first to become an officer in a family of enlisted men. But Mark had known from the get-go that that's what he wanted. Sam had only known he'd wanted to be an aviator. And to do that he had to become an officer, and to do that he had to get his college degree.

"You are the only pilot in your family, aren't you?"

He nodded.

"So I guess you didn't completely follow in your family's footsteps after all. How do they feel about you flying?"

"They support what I do."

"It must be nice having a family like that." Where had that wistful tone come from? She had no business being wistful. It made her sound like Little Orphan Annie—a poor waif to be pitied. No way was she falling into that role. She had her pride, after all. Not that it warmed her heart any, but that's what chocolate was for.

"Your family doesn't support your being a journalist?" Sam asked.

"I don't have any family," she said curtly.

"I'm sorry to hear that."

"Yeah, well." She shrugged, not wanting to sound defensive, either. "It's no big deal." She'd told herself and others that so many times over the years that you'd think she'd start to believe it by now. "Getting back to you, have you seen your family since your return to the States?"

"I took a brief personal leave to visit my parents

in Arizona. They retired there. Mark and his wife flew in so I saw them, too. As I told you last night, my older brother Justice trains Force Recon Marines. He's nearby in Virginia, so I've seen him, and Joe who's also stationed in the vicinity.''

Sam considered telling Cassie that he was supposed to baby-sit Joe's baby son tonight, but decided to surprise her with that information later. She'd been putting up so many barriers this morning that he didn't want her constructing even more.

If he could use the element of surprise to keep her off balance then he'd do that. Because he wanted to know the real Cassie Jones, the one hiding beneath the surface.

Not that she'd take the term "hiding" kindly. She prided herself on being tough but there was so much more to her. He'd met tough women who truly were hardened inside and out. Cassie wasn't one of those women.

He still didn't know what it was about her that so attracted him. Maybe the fact that she was a challenge. Unlike most other females, she hadn't made things easy for him. He hadn't actually had to chase after a member of the opposite sex since high school. All the Wilder brothers had a healthy dose of the Wilder charm, except perhaps for his oldest brother Justice who was more the silent, brooding type. But even that role had made Justice popular with women.

The thing was, Sam was growing weary of the dating game. Watching his older brothers fall in love and get married had at first been something to tease them about. But as he saw how happy they were in their new lives with their wives, he had to occasionally wonder what it would be like to experience that kind of love himself, to find the one woman you were meant to spend a lifetime with.

Oh, jeez, Striker was right. He was falling for Cassie. Like a ton of bricks.

The question was, what was he going to do about it? He needed to get things personal again. Not that he could do much, sitting there surrounded by other Marines. But he could say something to get things on track.

He leaned closer. "You know I keep thinking about Friday night."

She lifted her startled green eyes to meet his. "I thought we decided to forget about that kiss."

"Actually I was referring to your comments about feeling like Cinderella."

"Oh." Cassie felt like an idiot for being the one to refer to the kiss. Not that not talking about it kept it out of her mind. How could it when she'd just seen him working out?

"As I said Friday night, I think you're too proactive to sit around waiting for some prince to bring your shoe back to you."

"You've got that right. I wouldn't have expected that a Marine would be so into fairy tales."

"My mom read some of them to us when we were kids. She wanted us to have a rounded education."

"Yet you all ended up in the Marines. How does she feel about that?"

"My mom is great," Sam said simply.

Cassie tried to ignore the twinge in her heart. How nice it must be to say that and mean it.

Oh, Cassie had said the words about her own mom when she was younger, usually to keep the authorities at bay. If a teacher expressed concern at her mother never showing up at parent conferences, Cassie would sing her mom's praises, bragging about how hard she worked and how she couldn't take the time off to come to visit the school. And then they'd move on to another city, another school where Cassie would be the newcomer, the outsider, until the teacher there started asking too many questions or the landlord got fed up with the late rent payments. At which time, the entire process began again.

"How about Rapunzel?" Sam said.

"What?" Cassie blinked.

"Rapunzel. You know, the one with the long hair."

"My hair is short in case you hadn't noticed. Besides, wasn't she stuck in some stupid tower by a mean witch?"

"You're right. You'd have kicked that witch right out on her butt, right?"

"Affirmative," she returned with a grin.

"Actually I think you're most like Sleeping Beauty."

"Asleep all the time?"

"No, surrounded by thorns to keep others away."

He was getting a little too close for comfort here. In more ways than one. He was getting to her. Period. First with that fiery kiss the other night and now with his talk about aviator poetry and fairy-tale princesses. Time to call in reinforcements.

While Sam answered a phone call, Cassie stepped away to use her cell phone to call Al, her photographer. Well, actually the magazine's photographer, but she always made a point to ask for Al, because he was the best. And because he was a no-nonsense pro.

"Do you have any free time this afternoon to get

some shots of Captain Wilder for my story?'' she asked him.

"I could fit you in."

"Good."

"Why? What's up?"

"Nothing," she denied. "What makes you think anything is up?"

"Your voice. You sound different."

"Must be a bad cell phone connection," Cassie said.

"Yeah, must be."

"So you'll be here this afternoon? How soon?"

"I'm telling you, I'm hearing a definite sound of desperation in your voice. You can't blame that on a bad cell phone connection."

"Blame it on the Marine aviator," she muttered, eyeing Sam from across the room.

"What did he do?"

"Nothing. Nothing at all. You're imagining things, Al."

"Yeah, right. After all, I've got such an active imagination."

"You don't have any imagination at all. Usually."

"Right. Which is why I'm telling it like it is. You're sounding desperate, kid. Which makes me curious to see this Marine you're writing about. I'll be there in an hour."

"So you're the Marine. I've heard so much about you."

"So you're the photographer," Sam replied. "I'm sorry to say I haven't heard much about you, sir."

"That doesn't surprise me. Cassie never talks much. She lets her subjects do all the talking."

Sam quirked an eyebrow. "Subjects, sir?"

"The subjects of her stories. Not subjects as in royal subjects." Al laughed. "There's not a royal bone in Cassie's body. She's not the regal sort. She's too smart to be uptight and haughty."

"You know her well then, sir?"

Al nodded. "We've been working together for over a year now."

"Excuse me," Cassie said in exasperation. She hadn't imagined that the normally taciturn Al would suddenly turn so chatty. "You two don't have to talk about me as if I weren't here. In fact, you two don't have to talk about me at all."

"Why not?" Sam countered, using what she'd privately labeled his seductive hot-fudge voice. "I find you to be a fascinating subject."

"Because I'm not the focus of this story, you are."

"Cassie is right," Al said.

"Thank you." She smiled at him gratefully.

"But then Cassie is usually right," Al added.

"She told me she prefers to be called Cassandra," Sam confessed.

"So you call her Cassandra?" Al asked.

Sam shook his head.

Al laughed. "Oh, so you're the type that likes living dangerously then, huh?"

"I'm a Marine," Sam replied. "We're used to a little danger, sir."

Cassie cleared her throat and gave each man an irritated look. "Al, where do you suggest we shoot Sam?"

Sam winced. "Could you try not to sound so pleased when you use the word 'shoot'?"

"Should we shoot him inside or out?" Cassie continued.

"Either way sounds painful," Sam noted with a wry grin.

"No worries. You won't feel a thing," Al assured him with a matching grin.

Male bonding. Cassie couldn't believe it. Male bonding had run amok here, ruining her plans.

Al was supposed to be on her side. He was supposed to distract Sam. He wasn't supposed to gang up on her and he certainly wasn't supposed to make Sam grin. He looked much too sexy when he grinned. Dangerously sexy. Irresistibly sexy...

Shoot. She was a writer. She knew when not to use adverbs. Now Sam was messing up her vocabulary.

"Easy for you to say, sir," Sam was telling Al. "You're not the one having your photo taken."

"Surely a big bad Marine like you isn't afraid of a little tiny camera?" Cassie said.

"Hey, watch whose camera you're calling little," Al rumbled.

"You know how sensitive men are about things like size," Sam said in a solemn voice.

"I know how dumb they can be," she retorted.

"Ouch." Al winced sympathetically.

"If you two jocks are done comparing the size of your...equipment, maybe we could get some work done here."

"Yes, ma'am." Al saluted her smartly.

"Nice move, sir," Sam said.

"Send your thanks to the U.S. Army. I learned how to salute before dropping out of boot camp."

"Dropping out?" This was the first time Cassie had

heard any of this. "I didn't think you could drop out of boot camp."

"You can't," Sam said. "It's not like high school. But you can be dismissed if you fail to pass certain requirements or tests along the way."

"I wasn't very good at following orders," Al admitted.

"Yes, I'm learning that about you," Cassie said with a pointed look. Not that she was his boss or anything, but she thought they'd had an understanding. He was here to help her, not to be a hindrance.

Al just gave her one of his indecipherable smiles. With his white bushy hair and eyebrows, Al reminded her of one of those little white terrier dogs, the kind that was always pulling on the leash. Coming from Long Island he'd never been one to put a muzzle on his thoughts, always expressing them outright. But that had always been something that had endeared him to her in the past. He'd always been a staunch supporter of her work.

She had no idea what had come over him this afternoon. Some robotic clone must have taken over Al's body. A rebellious robotic clone into male bonding who was saying, "You can drop the sir stuff, Sam. Just call me Al."

"The photograph, Al, remember?" She gave him a pointed look. "Where do you think we should do the photo shoot?"

"I think I'll just tag along with you and Sam and take photos all the way. Some inside, some outside. Just don't take me to any restricted or classified areas, I wouldn't want to be taking pictures of something I shouldn't be."

"I thought maybe we should take some shots inside

the hangar, since Sam is an aviator.'' She was learning that they seemed to prefer that term to pilot. At least Sam seemed to use it more often.

''Good idea,'' Al agreed. ''Lead on, oh fearless reporter.''

And so they all headed out to the helicopter hangar. ''You'll need to take photos out here on the tarmac rather than inside because of security concerns.''

''This is the squadron that ferries the President around,'' Cassie told Al. ''They also test and evaluate military helicopters here.''

Al nodded his understanding. ''I've got a digital camera so I can show you the shot after I've taken it, to make sure it comes out right.''

''Sounds like a plan,'' Sam agreed.

''Okay, give me one of those rough-tough-can't-get-enough Marine looks,'' Al instructed Sam. ''Show me your battle face.''

Cassie was amazed at the way Sam's expression changed, wiped clean of emotion. Even his eyes became threatening while displaying a world-weary knowledge that she found disconcerting. The charming sexy man she'd spent so many hours with had been transformed into a dangerous warrior.

''Good, good,'' Al was saying enthusiastically as he moved around Sam, using different angles.

''You don't wear that uniform when you fly, do you?''

''No, sir.''

''Then maybe you should be wearing your aviator uniform, or whatever you call it,'' Al suggested.

Sam didn't appear thrilled at the idea. ''I'd need to get that cleared with a Public Affairs officer.''

''Fine. You go ahead and do that,'' Cassie said,

eager to get some time alone with her photographer to set matters straight. "Al and I will wait right here for you."

"I can't leave you here unescorted," Sam replied before calling over a private. "Stay with Ms. Jones and her photographer until my return."

"Yes, sir. Understood, sir."

Taking Al by the arm, Cassie moved out of earshot of the private. "What was all that about?"

Al blinked at her. "All what?"

"All that bonding with Sam. You're not supposed to bond with him."

"I'm not? You weren't real clear on your instructions, Cassie."

"You're supposed to be my friend."

"I am your friend. Which is why I'm gonna show you my last shot." He held the digital camera up so she could see the display screen. He'd somehow gotten her in the shot as well as Sam.

"The camera doesn't lie," he said. His voice softened as he added, "It's there on your face, Cassie."

"What is?"

"The fact that you're falling for this Marine."

Chapter Seven

"You're crazy, Al." Cassie's voice was shaken. "There's no way I'd be that stupid."

Al shook his head sadly. "I'll say it again, Cassie. The camera doesn't lie."

"Maybe not, but it fibs. That sappy look on my face must have been some trick of the lighting. Or maybe I was thinking of some other guy."

"What other guy?" Al frowned. "You haven't been seeing anyone steadily."

"What are you? My mother?"

"No, but if she were here, she'd tell you…"

"She'd tell me to go buy her more booze," Cassie said unsteadily. "That was always her top priority. Having enough alcohol."

"Jeez, kid, I had no idea. You never talk about your parents."

"Yeah, well now you know why. Please, forget I said anything about it," she said, feeling hot with embarrassment at her lapse. She was usually so careful not to let anything slip about her past. After all, she'd had years of experience at keeping secrets. "I'd rather concentrate on the here and now. Which brings me to Sonya. I ran into her at a charity event Friday night."

"Oh, yeah? And what did she have to say for herself?"

"She accused me of using my looks in order to get this feature story. She also said that Phil only gave me this assignment because I colored my hair and changed my appearance."

"Well, you did say that you wanted more attention," Al reminded her with a grin. "I just don't think you meant for it to come from the Reptile Woman."

"I never did hear how she got that nickname."

"Are you kidding? She should be on every reptile's hit list. She's got more reptile shoes and bags and stuff than you can shake a stick or a snake at. Not that I'm any expert on women's shoes or bags," Al added defensively. "I know how these rumors get started…"

"So do I. Which is why I wasn't pleased to hear Sonya telling me that everyone in the office is talking about me."

"Well, you did want to be a whiplash blonde, which means you're gonna get attention."

"Are people at work saying that I only got this assignment because of my looks?"

"Of course not."

"You'd tell me if they were?"

"Yes. Why did you take her bait this way?"

She shrugged. "I guess because the truth is that people do treat me differently now that I look different."

"I don't."

"I wouldn't say that. I called you out here for some moral support and instead you sided with Sam."

"Moral support, huh? Gee, and here I thought I was out here for a photo shoot."

"That, too. You know what I mean."

"Sam and I were just teasing you. I've teased you before."

"I know."

"So what's the big deal now all of a sudden?" She shrugged.

"Unless Sam is the big deal," Al noted astutely. "Is he?"

"He wouldn't look twice at me if I hadn't changed my looks."

"You can't know that for sure."

"Yes, I can. You were at that press conference when he first returned to the States. He looked right past me."

"Hey, give the guy a break, would you? He'd just saved a dozen people's lives by landing that plane safely during the surveillance flight in the Middle East a few days before that press conference. He didn't look all that comfortable with being in the spotlight if you ask me."

"See, this is what I was talking about. You're taking his side."

"Hey, I didn't realize you two were on opposite sides. And judging from the look on your face when I took that candid photo, I'd say that there's more to your reaction to him than irritation at his ignoring you at his press conference. I said it before and I'll say it again, you're falling for the guy."

"I am not! Stop saying that. You're only making things worse."

"What would be so bad about falling for him? Is he involved with someone else, is that it?"

"They say he has a Teflon heart. And do you know why they say that? Because no woman ever sticks very long. Sh-hh," she hissed. "Here he comes. Act natural."

"I always act natural," Al said. "You're the one acting weird."

"Public Affairs has a photo of me in my flight suit," Sam said, handing it over. "They prefer you use this one."

"It's a standard headshot," Al rumbled. "No originality."

Cassie looked at the photo Al held, wiping out his words as he continued to critique its lighting and composition. Instead she focused on the image of Sam wearing a flight suit, holding a helmet in one arm and smiling at the camera. His arresting blue eyes were squinted a bit against the sunlight while the laugh lines fanned out at their corners.

It was just a photograph, and Al was right, a standard one at that. Yet it had the power to make her heart beat faster and her knees to tremble. And standing only a few feet away was the real thing—Sam in reality, Sam in the flesh.

Cassie closed her eyes and saw a mental snapshot of him earlier that morning, working out in the gym. His tank top had displayed his compact yet powerful shoulders and muscular arms even more than the T-shirt he'd worn for their run together.

What was happening to her? She'd never been the type to fall for a wickedly handsome face and sexy body before. What was wrong with her?

Al couldn't be right. She couldn't be falling for Sam.

For one thing, it would be very unprofessional of her to get personally involved with the subject of one of her stories. Wouldn't it? The possibility had never even arisen before. She'd always liked talking to the people she interviewed, enjoyed hearing their stories, finding out what made them tick.

But Sam was different. The more time she spent with him, the more she discovered that he wasn't the cocky flyboy she'd expected. He was smart, he was funny, he had a way of making her feel special. The bottom line was that he was far more dangerous to her peace of mind than she'd ever anticipated.

Here she'd been so confident when she'd first arrived at Quantico that she was the woman who could handle this sexy Marine. And now look at her. Weak at the knees over a stupid photograph, fantasizing about him wearing that tank top and shorts. She was definitely in trouble here.

Maybe it was time to gain a little perspective on this case. Time for her to get a little distance. But how was she supposed to do that when her assignment was to stay by his side, sticking to him like a shadow?

Cassie was reminded of the little sign she had propped on her desk; Nobody Said It Would Be Easy But This Is Ridiculous. Yep, that was pretty much her life in a nutshell. Which meant she should be a pro at handling tough situations.

The problem wasn't the tough situation, it was the tough and handsome Marine causing the situation.

''Well, I guess that's all the damage I can do here today,'' Al declared.

It was his customary comment at the end of a photo

shoot but today it had special meaning. For his comments about Cassie's feeling for Sam had shaken her deeply, as much as she was striving to hide it.

She watched Sam check the time on his watch before speaking to Al.

"I thought I'd take Cassie out to a great authentic Mexican restaurant I know," Sam said. "You're welcome to come along if you'd like, Al."

Al paused a second as if considering. Then his pager went off. "I'm needed back at the magazine," he said. "Looks like you'll be on your own tonight, kid," he told Cassie.

"She won't be on her own, I'll be with her," Sam said with a proprietary air that would have driven her up the wall had any other man used it. But now it made her feel oddly protected.

Don't get used to it, she warned herself. This situation is only temporary. Once you're done researching this story, you'll move on to another feature and Sam will move on to another woman.

"Be sure you get her home at a reasonable hour," Al said, the laughter in his voice belying his attempt at a fatherly tone.

"Yes, sir."

"Nice performance," Cassie noted mockingly. "But I'm going to have to deduct points for talking about me as if I weren't here."

Al just laughed. "Have fun tonight, Cassie."

"I'm sure I will," she automatically replied.

But not too much fun, she silently warned herself. Don't have too much fun with Sam, don't get used to being with him and whatever you do, do not fall in love with him.

* * *

"You seem unusually quiet this evening," Sam said after placing their order at the little Mexican café he'd taken her to. They were seated at a ranchero-style wooden table while Mexican ballads softly played in the background. Sam had changed out of his uniform into more casual clothes. He was pure muscle poured into black jeans and a black T-shirt.

"I was just thinking about the feature story, different angles for an opening hook, that sort of thing," she fibbed. "Nothing you'd be interested in."

"I'm interested in everything about you."

"Yeah, right," she scoffed with a laugh.

"Why do you do that?"

"Do what?" She paused in the middle of dipping a tortilla chip in the spicy salsa that had been placed on their table when they'd first arrived.

"Act as if you don't believe what I'm saying to you."

"I don't believe it."

"You think I'm feeding you some line?"

"I think you've made a career out of charming women. In between doing your Marine thing."

Cassie expected him to get angry with her. But Sam never did what she expected, drat him. He merely shook his head and reached for a tortilla chip...just as she was reaching for one. It wasn't until his fingers brushed hers that she realized what was going on.

By then it was too late. Awareness hummed from the point where their fingers touched, instantly flowing through her entire body with the potent warmth of jalapeño peppers.

She refused to back down. Pulling her hand away would only show him how deeply he affected her. So she didn't move. She even met his gaze head-on, refusing to turn away from the warmth in his dark blue eyes.

Sam had a way of looking at a woman as if she were the only female on the planet that could possibly hold any interest for him. Cassie reminded herself that he probably looked at every woman that way while he was with them, making each one of them feel special.

But telling herself these things didn't seem to matter to her heart, which was beating faster than a journalist's heart should. A journalist's heart should be objective, interested in discovering the truth not in discovering the feel of Sam's hands on her body. That would not be a good thing.

Well, actually, it might be an incredible thing while it lasted…if she was the kind of woman interested in one-night stands. But she wasn't.

Which brought her back to the fact that none of this was real. Sam's interest in her wasn't real, because he didn't know or see the real her. She was an imposter parading around as a confident whiplash blonde when inside she was the same out-of-step loner she'd always been. She was still a virgin, for heaven's sake. Not a Tough Chick at all.

Cassie hastily pulled her hand away, then tried to cover her nervous reaction with a joke. "Hey, if you want that tortilla chip that badly, you go ahead and have it." She focused her attention on the orange-and-red walls and terra-cotta floor. The festive decor created a warm atmosphere. Of course, Sam's meaningful looks in her direction created an even hotter atmosphere, but she couldn't let him know that. "This is a nice place."

"I'm glad you like it. I hope everything is spicy enough for you."

"I'm sure it will be. So what's on the agenda for tonight? You never did tell me what you have planned."

"I wanted to surprise you."

"I'm not real big on surprises." Cassie had had enough of them growing up, never knowing what shape her mother would be in when Cassie came home from school.

"That surprises me. I would have thought a Tough Chick like you would thrive on adventure and surprises."

"I can handle adventure just fine."

"I'm glad to hear that. Because tonight we're in for an adventure…in baby-sitting."

"Isn't that the title of a movie?"

"It's a description of our evening."

"Baby-sitting?"

"That's right. Baby-sitting my ten-month-old nephew Matt."

Cassie tried telling herself that this could be a good thing, a chance for her to see Sam interacting with his family, a nice addition to her feature story. But inside she was nervous. She had no experience with baby-sitting. No experience with babies, period.

Not a problem. You're just here to observe, not to participate, she reminded herself.

"Sounds like fun," she lied. "Why didn't you tell me about this earlier?"

"Like I said, I wanted to surprise you. And, frankly, I wasn't sure how you'd react to the news."

"React? I'm just here to take notes on your life."

She tapped her pen on her small spiral notebook to reinforce that notion.

"Just here to take notes, huh?"

She nodded firmly.

He reached across the table to brush one long lean finger over the back of her hand. There was no way such a simple touch should have generated so much sexual energy, but it did. "Tell me about it."

"About what?" Her voice was husky. Must be the spicy salsa.

"About your notes. What are you writing?"

"I'm not writing anything at the moment." She pulled her hand away, steadying it in her lap before reaching out to sip her margarita. "Mmm, they use fresh lime to make these."

His gaze shifted to her lips. "Fresh is always better."

The deep blue of his eyes had darkened to nearly black with the intensity of his look. The blatant appreciation she saw there nearly took her breath away.

"Here you go," their waiter said, interrupting the moment. "*Guero chile relleño* for you, *señor,* and *enchiladas con mole* for the *señorita.* Can I get you anything else? No? Then enjoy your meal."

And she did enjoy her meal. The rolled corn tortilla stuffed with chicken was delicious.

"Want a taste of mine?" Sam tempted her by holding up a plump gulf shrimp.

But it was the challenge in his voice that made her reply, "Sure. Why not?"

Instead of handing her the shrimp, he moved it to her mouth. "Take a bite."

She did, almost nipping his fingers in the process.

He grinned at her. "Nice move."

"You want to be careful feeding Tough Chicks," Cassie warned him. "We've been known to bite when provoked."

"I'm counting on that," he murmured.

"Doesn't anything faze you, Captain?"

"Being unfazed is part of my training. However, seeing you in that dress Friday night certainly...fazed me."

"It was the first time I'd ever worn that dress." Now why had she confessed that?

"I'm glad and honored to be the first man to see you wearing it."

"You've definitely got a way with words, but I'm sure you've been told that before."

"I can't have much of a way with words if you don't believe what I say."

"I believe that you're a charmer. But there's really no need to practice your charms on me. I'm just here to write this story." She patted her notebook. "And once it's done, I'll be out of your hair."

"What if I like having you in my hair?"

His question caught her by surprise. She didn't know what to say. Was that why he'd said it? "Come on, Sam. No one enjoys having a reporter following them around twelve hours or more a day."

"I wasn't talking about you as a reporter, I was talking about you as a woman."

"You only know me as a reporter, you don't know me as a woman. It's safer this way."

"Safer?" He raised one dark eyebrow. "Safer for whom?"

"For both of us."

"I seem to recall you telling me that first night we spent together that you enjoyed taking risks. In fact, you told me you take risks all the time, that if you don't take risks you'll never succeed.''

"Some kind of risks are worth taking, others aren't.''

"Meaning what? That you don't take romantic risks?''

"Bingo.''

"Why not?'' Sam demanded. "What are you afraid of?''

She was afraid of becoming like her mother, a woman who'd depended utterly on a man to make her happy and when he'd died, she'd never gotten over it, never stopped blaming him for abandoning her and ruining her happiness, driving her to forget her problems in a bottle of alcohol.

One of Cassie's fears was that she'd become her mother, which was why she always limited her own alcoholic intake to an occasional drink.

Her other fear ran even deeper than that, so deep that it was an integral part of her very being. The fear that since her own mother couldn't love her, that no one could ever love her.

"What am I afraid of?'' she said. "How about Marine pilots too darn sure of their own attractiveness for their own good?''

"So you think I'm attractive?''

She rolled her eyes. "Oh, please. As if you don't already know the answer to that one. I'm sure you know you're attractive.''

"I was talking about you, about what *you* think.''

"Why should that matter to you?''

"It does.''

"Well, it shouldn't,'' she retorted.

"Why not?''

"Listen, I'm the one who's supposed to be asking the questions."

"Then go ahead. Ask me anything you want," he told her.

She tried to come up with something that would shake that confidence of his, but in the end she didn't have the heart for it. "Are you going to finish that dessert all by yourself?"

He was surprised. "I thought you didn't want any dessert."

"I changed my mind."

"A woman's prerogative. I'm more than happy to share."

"Good." She reached for her unused coffee spoon and eagerly dug into the ice cream concoction, getting plenty of cinnamon, chocolate, hot fudge and toasted coconut.

He had to laugh at her enthusiasm. But as they neared his brother's house thirty minutes later, she was no longer laughing. She was getting more and more tense by the minute. They'd agreed to drive together in his rented car. Darkness was falling with the suddenness so common in the fall.

"You've gone all quiet on me again," Sam noted.

"I feel it only fair to warn you that I know nothing about kids." Her voice sounded strained.

"You were one once," Sam reminded her.

"Not really," Cassie replied.

"What do you mean?"

"I mean that I was pretty much responsible for myself growing up."

"What about your parents?"

"My father died shortly after I was born so I have no memory of him at all."

"What about your mom?"

"My earliest memory of my mother is of her lying on the couch with a bottle of alcohol on the floor beside her. I was hungry, but I couldn't wake her up to make anything to eat. So I did it myself. From that day on I pretty much did most things myself, including taking care of her." The words kept tumbling out. "She never meant to get drunk again, but she did. Over and over again. So I learned early how to cope on my own. Other kids were out playing while I was trying to figure out how to make the little money my mom had stretch to pay the rent and pay for food. Writing was my escape, my way out of the situation I was in. That's how I survived. My mom died when I was eighteen and I was alone."

She didn't notice that they'd reached their destination until Sam turned to her in the darkness of his car. Taking her in his arms, he whispered, "It's okay. You're not alone anymore."

Chapter Eight

"Did you hear what I said?" Sam spoke the words against the top of her head, his voice muffled. "I said you're not alone anymore."

Cassie wanted to believe him, wanted it so much that it almost hurt. But she was afraid, afraid to put her trust in someone else. Yes, she was a risk taker, but in this case the risk was so great.

But the reward would be great, as well.

She wavered, more tempted than she'd ever been in her entire life to give in. His arms provided such a warm shelter. But the emotional risk was still so high.

As if sensing her uncertainty, Sam said, "Just leave yourself open to possibilities, okay?"

"Okay." Possibilities. She could handle possibilities.

"Okay." He kissed the top of her head and reluctantly released her from his embrace. "We'd better get in there or my nosy brother will come out here looking for us."

Cassie almost hopped out of the car in her eagerness to avoid that possibility. The compact ranch house had a small porch with the light on, illuminating a lime-green wicker rocking chair sporting a cheerful gingham pillow. A series of red geraniums in terra-cotta pots lined the path leading to the front door.

Taking her hand firmly in his, Sam gave her fingers a reassuring squeeze before ringing the bell.

A moment later the door was opened by a man who could have been a dead ringer for a younger Mel Gibson—the same square jaw and vivid blue eyes. He was wearing black slacks and a navy blue shirt. He was also staring at them with surprise. ''What are you doing here?''

''Very funny.'' Sam rolled his eyes as he guided Cassie inside.

She took note of a cozy-looking living room before Sam told her, ''I should warn you that my brother Joe is the worst practical joker.''

''Hey, I'll have you know that I'm a world-class practical joker,'' Joe declared.

''You're not bragging about putting Heat in your brothers' jock straps again, are you?'' his wife demanded. With her dark brown shoulder-length hair and sparkling brown eyes, she looked like the girl-next-door. While attractive enough, she certainly wasn't as good-looking as her dashing husband. But there was no mistaking the loving glances they exchanged. In her arms was a chubby baby with rosy cheeks and blue eyes.

''No, I wasn't bragging about that,'' Joe denied. ''Actually that was a practical joke I stole from my good buddy Curt. Therefore I wouldn't want to take credit for coming up with it myself. That would be plagiarism, which I'm sure a writer like you knows would be a bad thing.'' He directed this last sentence to Cassie.

''Yes, indeed,'' she noted with a grin. His teasing was infectious.

''I'm Prudence Wilder, by the way.'' She handed the baby to her husband before holding out a hand to Cassie. ''Welcome to our home. Come and make yourselves comfortable.''

Once the belated greetings were over with Joe said, ''So you're doing a story on my baby brother here, huh? Well, if you want any of the dirt on this guy, you just come to me.''

''Really? Dirt, huh? Like what?''

''Nothing.'' Sam shot a warning glare at his older brother. ''Joe is full of hot air.''

''No, that would be little Matt here,'' Joe replied, jiggling the baby propped on his shoulder. ''He's the one full of hot air. The kid has been burping thunderclaps all day. Me, I'm a responsible father and purveyor of truths.''

''And if you believe that, I've got some land in Arizona to sell you,'' Sam said.

''I didn't know you were going into real estate,'' Joe countered.

Cassie loved having Sam be the target of teasing for a change, having *him* be the one discomfited.

''So did you get the naked photos of Sam for your story yet?'' Joe inquired casually.

Cassie's eyes widened. ''Naked photos?''

''I was a baby at the time,'' Sam said.

''Our mom took naked baby photos as well as a few embarrassing childhood shots of all of us,'' Joe explained. "I swear she planned even then on using them on us when we grew up, to keep us in our places."

"I haven't spoken to your mother," Cassie said.

"You should," Joe replied.

She probably should. But mothers were a bit of a touchy subject with her at the moment. Especially after what she'd just confessed to Sam in the car. She still didn't know what had made her do that.

It wasn't like her at all. She never talked about it to anyone. Until today, when she'd let something slip while talking to Al and then had that meltdown moment in the car with Sam.

She had to get her act together here.

"Okay, you know the baby-sitting rules," Joe was saying. "No using the baby as a football, no stealing the kid's strained pea baby food, and no making out on the couch."

Sam was used to his brother's teasing ways, but he worried about what Cassie would think. "Ignore him," he said.

"Easier said than done," Prudence noted with a smile. "You Wilder men are very hard to ignore, no matter how much a woman might want to."

"Why would any woman want to ignore us?" Joe demanded.

Prudence just rolled her eyes and shared a woman-to-woman look with Cassie. "We'd better go or we'll be late for our dinner reservations. I've written down our cell phone number. The name of the restaurant along with its number. And Joe's pager number." She handed the information over to Cassie. "If you need to call us…"

"They won't. Sam has taken care of Matt before, just a few weeks ago."

"I know," Prudence said. "I'm just saying that if an emergency should arise then they should contact us."

"Otherwise they shouldn't contact us," Joe said with a grin. "Come on, let's go."

The next thing Cassie knew, he'd handed the baby to her instead of to Sam.

She froze but no one seemed to notice. She'd never handled a baby before. Weren't you supposed to support their head or something? What was that slimy stuff coming out of his mouth? Was he about to do something gross?

"Here." She turned to hand the baby over to Sam but he was by the door, seeing his brother and sister-in-law out.

Leaning back against the closed door, Sam gave her one of his irresistible smiles. "Ah, alone at last."

She rushed toward him so fast he almost bumped into her when he moved away from the door. "Here, you take him." Darn, she sounded panicked. She'd so wanted to sound nonchalant. "I mean, he's your nephew, you should hold him. He doesn't know me from Adam." There, that explanation sounded very calm and logical. Nice going, she congratulated herself.

"That's okay, you keep him. Matt seems to like you."

She hadn't seen his refusal to take the baby coming at all. The kid was getting heavy, holding him the way she was with her hands under his baby armpits. "No, I'm sure he likes you better. And look, I think he's going to cry."

Thankfully, Sam finally took Matt from her, holding him in his arms the way a receiver would hold a ball in a football game. Cassie actually had more experience with football than she did with babies.

"What's the matter, buddy?" Sam rocked him a bit.

"Is that stuff supposed to be coming out of his mouth that way?"

"Sure. He's just drooling." Sam reached for a towel laying on the couch where Joe had left it.

"Why is he making that face?"

"What face? He looks like this all the time."

"I told you I didn't have much experience with kids."

"This is your chance to change that. Here, you hold him again."

She shook her head.

"Don't tell me you're afraid of a little baby? A Tough Chick like you? Come on, Cassie." Sam used his best coaxing voice and she had to admit it was pretty darn effective. "He won't bite you. He doesn't have many teeth yet. In fact, I'm not sure he has any. Want to open his mouth up so we can take a look?"

"No, I do not want to do any such thing. I'm sure he wouldn't appreciate that, either."

"Party pooper," Sam rumbled.

There he was, making her smile again. The man was way too...too everything. Too good to be true.

"Maybe he's hungry. Come on, let's go in the kitchen and feed him. You might want to stay back for this event, it can get messy."

That was an understatement if she'd ever heard one she noted a few minutes later as Sam wiped mashed peas from his cheek.

"No spitting, mister. That's an order." Although Sam's voice was firm, it lacked the bite of authority he used when giving orders to someone under his command.

"You look good in green," she told him with a grin. "I'd say that color pretty much matches your service uniform shirt color. Maybe I should use mashed peas instead of khaki as a description in my article."

"I'm sure the Marine Corps would not be pleased to see our outstanding uniforms likened to mashed peas."

"Not manly enough, huh?"

"Not at all." Sam held a spoon of vile-looking stuff to baby Matt's mouth. "And we Wilder men like to be manly, right buddy?"

Splat.

This time Matt hit the spoon with his gaily flailing hands, sending its contents flying in the air where it landed in the middle of Sam's forehead.

Cassie cracked up.

"Ignore her," Sam told Matt as he wiped the gook from his face. "She doesn't understand that you were just showing off your newfound manual dexterity. This time let's show her how it should be done." He dipped the tiny spoon in the glass jar again. "Okay, here it comes, buddy."

"Maybe it would help if you made airplane noises," she suggested. "I've seen people do that on TV."

"Okay, it's worth a try." Sam gave his best Chinook helicopter impersonation while keeping a running dialogue. "The helo is down, ramp is down, move out…" He moved the spoon closer. "The firing teams have poured out of the helo, forming a semi-circular hasty defense line around our position. Time to load 'em up, buddy.''

But baby Matt had other ideas. Another swat of his hand and the food was airborne again.

"Incoming," Sam shouted, ducking this time.

Cassie wasn't as lucky.

"We have a direct hit on the lovely lady's cheek," he noted, looking over his shoulder. "Bad baby."

Matt just chortled happily and drooled some more.

"Here, let me help you." Sam dumped the spoon and scooted his chair closer to hers.

Sam cupped Cassie's face with one hand while he used the other to dab at her cheek with a kitchen towel. His touch was incredibly gentle for such a strong man. An all-too-familiar warmth rushed through her. She experienced this reluctant excitement whenever his hand grazed hers, whenever his body brushed against hers, whenever he looked at her in a way that told her he wanted her.

He was so close she could see the ring around the blue iris in his eyes. Which meant he was close enough to see her imperfections. She nervously shied away.

"That's okay." She grabbed the towel from him and wiped the remaining baby food from her face. "I'm fine now."

"You sure?" His voice was quiet, as if he sensed that there was more going on with her than met the eye.

"Positive. I think I'll move a little further back from the front lines, however." She got up and moved her chair closer to the fridge and farther away from him and Matt. "There, that's better."

She wished she could open the freezer and stick her head inside. Maybe that would cool her off.

Why had she acted like a nervous adolescent when he'd touched her? While it was true that she was a virgin, she had had several boyfriends, she had been kissed and touched in a passionate way by a man. But not touched by blinding passion. And she'd never been filled with a reckless need like this before.

But her passion was matched by a relentless fear. Cassie had never worried what those previous men in her life had thought of her. She hadn't cared. They could take her as she was or they could leave.

But everything was different now. Now she was a whiplash blonde, a Tough Chick who got attention. The problem was that she didn't know what to do with that attention.

No, that wasn't right. She knew what she wanted to do. She wanted to stay in Sam's arms forever.

This isn't real, that inner voice of fear whispered yet again inside her head. *Sam isn't attracted to the real you. You heard what Sonya said the other night. Sam wouldn't give the real you a second glance. Don't be fooled.*

"You're so far away you're going to need binoculars to see what's going on over here," Sam complained.

"I can see just fine from here."

The distance didn't help as much as she'd hoped it would. She could indeed see just fine from where she was, could see the wonderful way Sam handled baby Matt, the ease with which he cared for him, the love he showed him.

"You definitely need a bath after that workout,"

Sam told Matt. "I'm going to need your help, Cassie," he added.

The words warmed her heart. Sam needed her.

A powerful prospect, even if only a temporary one. Because a man like Sam didn't really need anyone or anything. As a Marine he was capable of depending solely on himself.

But then baby-bath giving probably wasn't part of standard Marine Corps training.

"You have given him a bath before, haven't you?" Cassie asked.

"Come on, he's a baby. How hard can it be?"

They soon found out. They were both wet from head to waist as baby Matt cheerfully smacked his hands in the water in the baby-bath container set on the floor in his room.

Sam had suggested putting the container on the changing table but they'd opted for the floor when Matt almost kicked the container off the table as they tried to put him in it.

Cassie had once written an article on baby safety several years ago, parts of which were coming back to her. Something about a baby being able to drown in only a few inches of water kept coming back to haunt her, which meant either she or Sam was holding the baby upright at all times while the other washed him with a soft baby washcloth and baby wash.

Once Matt was out of the water, Sam efficiently diapered him before handing him over to her.

"Here," Sam said, "you hold him on your lap and finish drying him off while I go get rid of this water before he does any more damage."

Cassie sat on the floor, her long skirt spread out around her, her red T-shirt still damp, with baby Matt sitting on a towel spread across her lap. He was a cute baby as far as babies went. And he laughed and grinned at her. Oh, yes, he definitely had the Wilder grin.

"You're going to grow up to be a charmer just like your daddy and uncle, aren't you? Well, don't bother using that baby charm on me, buddy." She borrowed Sam's nickname. "I'm immune to it. Really I am. Go ahead, try and charm me."

He reached for her hand and stuck her finger in his mouth.

"He has good taste in women," Sam noted wryly.

"Or do women just taste good to him? He's gnawing on my finger."

"Good thing he doesn't have many teeth then."

"Now he's sucking on it."

"I'm jealous."

The idea of Sam sucking on her fingers made her all hot and bothered inside. Outside she remained relatively calm, considering she had a baby on her lap. Actually she was kind of getting used to it. Sam had handed the baby over to her several times while cleaning up the mess in the kitchen and while getting his bath ready. As with anything, practice made perfect. And while she was still far from perfect, she was beginning to feel something…something she couldn't quite put her finger on, something that gave her heart a funny little ache.

"He likes you," Sam said.

"You think so?"

"I know so. Want to hold him while he gets his bottle?"

Sam was giving her the option of saying no.

"You say you're a woman who likes taking risks," he reminded her.

"Fine. I'll hold him. Where should I sit?"

"In the rocking chair in the corner."

Sam showed her how and Matt showed her, as well, reaching with his little hands. They were such perfect things, five little fingers complete with tiny fingernails. His skin was so soft. And his gaze so trusting as he looked up at her.

When Matt was done with his bottle, Sam burped him and placed him back in her lap, which was clearly where he wanted to be.

"Story time is next on the agenda," Sam announced.

"What's the selection tonight?" she teased him. "The history of the Marine Corps? Of Quantico? How a soldier saved the world?"

"How about the story of the perfect Marine?"

"Your autobiography?"

"No, the story of Master Gunnery Sergeant Leland 'Lou' Diamond. Fought in two world wars. Early in his career he was dubbed 'The Honker' due to his incredible booming voice which could be heard above all other noises, even in combat. There's one story about him lobbing a mortar shell down the smoke-stack of an offshore Japanese cruiser on a dare from a fellow Marine that's a real winner..."

"And he lived happily ever after," Cassie hastily inserted with a meaningful look in Sam's direction. "I don't think Matt needs to hear about mortar shells. Let's read a story about Winnie-the-Pooh instead."

"Party pooh-per. Get it?" Sam was as pleased with himself as any little kid.

"Yes, and you're going to get it, next time Matt needs his diaper changed."

"Dumpy Diapers can't need changing yet. I just changed him a few minutes ago."

"He doesn't need changing yet, but he will."

"Sure you don't want me to show you how to do that?"

"Positive."

"Wimp."

She waved his words aside as if they were nothing more than pesky insects. "You're not daring me into it."

"Wimp, wimp, wimp." Then Sam spoke to the baby. "Repeat after me, Dumpy Diapers. Wimp, wimp, wimp."

"Your brother and sister-in-law would be so pleased to hear you teaching him his first word."

Sam laughed. "I can picture it now. My brother coaxing Daddy out of his kid and instead Dumpy Diapers says 'wimp.' I love it."

"Well, I don't, so forget about it. Here, help me read *Winnie-the-Pooh*. You can be Piglet."

"I don't want to be Piglet. He's a whiner. No way am I doing Piglet. I want to be Tigger. Now that's a guy with attitude."

"Attitude and not a lot of smarts. You're right," she teased Sam. "Suits you to a T."

"Watch out, I'm armed and dangerous." He wielded a baby pillow.

"You wouldn't hit a woman with a baby on her lap."

"No, but I'd kiss her."

A second later he swooped down to do just that,

tipping her chin up to kiss her firmly on the lips. He lingered just long enough for her to want more.

But baby Matt, aka Dumpy Diapers, had other ideas, grabbing hold of Sam's black T-shirt to try to pull himself upright.

Startled, Sam backed away. "Did you see that? He was trying to stand up."

"My lap isn't the best place to be doing that." Cassie tightened her hold on the baby. "What if he falls?"

"You won't let him fall."

"You've got that right. So no more distracting me, understood?"

His raised eyebrow made her realize how his mannerisms were becoming endearingly familiar to her. Raising one eyebrow produced his Who Me? look. She'd also learned to read the laughter in his blue eyes before she heard it in his voice. And she'd learned that she was incredibly vulnerable to this man's particular brand of charm.

"Let's just focus on reading *Winnie-the-Pooh*, okay?" The words were meant as much for herself as for Sam.

Baby Matt loved being read to, and wasn't happy hearing just one book and looking at the illustrations. He wanted another, and another.

"Time for bed," Sam announced.

But baby Matt had other ideas. Once tucked in, he kicked his covers off and started crying.

"It's okay, he'll settle down in a minute or two," Sam said, taking her by the arm and leading her out of the room.

But Matt didn't stop. Cassie couldn't bear to just leave him like that. She felt the sting of tears in her own eyes as she heard the sound of his sobs increasing. She didn't even last five minutes before entering his room.

"It's okay." Her heart ached as the baby held out his little arms to her. "I'm here. We didn't abandon—" Her voice caught. "We didn't abandon you."

Sam heard the catch in her voice and kicked himself for not recognizing the reason for it earlier. Cassie had just told him in the car about her mom. And while her mom hadn't physically abandoned her, she had emotionally—never being there for Cassie growing up.

Sam knew the devastating effects alcoholism could have on families. He'd seen the results when he'd worked with new recruits, many of whom came from single-parent homes, many of whom had parents addicted to drugs or alcohol. They came to the Marine Corps looking for a sense of belonging. They also received the discipline that had often been lacking in their own lives.

Cassie didn't lack discipline. She was an incredibly hard worker. And she never did anything halfway. It was all or nothing with her.

Which made him wonder what making love with her would be like. It had taken all his considerable self-discipline to pull away after kissing her earlier. He'd only meant to tease her, but the instant his lips touched hers he felt the magnetic pull.

Cassie was special. He watched her soothing Matt, her features softened in the warm glow of the clown night-light plugged into the wall nearby. She rocked Matt, her voice a softly soothing sound.

Sam imagined what it would be like, coming home and finding her sitting in *their* home, rocking *their* baby on her lap. He'd never wondered about that kind of thing before. Oh, maybe long-term, as some kind of concept in his distant future. He knew he wanted kids.

But he'd never pictured one specific woman in the role before. And that freaked him a bit. Because it seemed to indicate that his feelings for her weren't just sexual, there was something more going on here.

Did she feel it, too? When she'd watched him in the kitchen earlier feeding Matt, had she considered the possibility of them being together, of her having his baby?

Maybe it was just being around a baby? Maybe they had that effect on couples. A couple. Him and Cassie. A couple. He liked the sound of that.

He also liked the way she looked, sitting there half asleep herself. Her rocking motion had not only sent Matt to dreamland, it had also worked on her, as well.

Moving closer, Sam carefully removed Matt and returned him to his crib, where he settled without a peep. Then he turned back to Cassie, who was blinking at him sleepily. She stood and swayed a bit.

Sam immediately scooped her up into his arms and carried her out of the room. Startled, she wrapped her arms around his neck. He liked the way she felt against him, the way her breasts brushed against his chest. He liked it so much that when they reached the living room, he wasn't in any hurry to put her down, lowering her to her feet with slow deliberation, allowing her body to slide against his, inch by inch.

He saw by the flare in her green eyes that she felt the chemistry, too.

"The baby..." she whispered.

"Is sleeping. The baby monitor is on." Sam nodded toward the white plastic receiver on the end table. "So we can hear him if he cries. But he won't cry. *I* might, though, if I don't kiss you right now."

Sam swiftly covered her mouth with his own. Her parted lips were ready for him, welcoming him with undisguised eagerness. Intoxicating passion flowed through her veins, melting any idea of resistance. This was too good to defy, too intense to deny.

The kiss was just as incendiary as the one they'd shared beneath that oak tree near her apartment building. Maybe even more so, because now they were alone together, free to explore and pursue.

He was her black knight and he'd come to lift her from a world without magic, without love. He showed her the marvels to be had, to be savored, to be devoured—nibbling at her lips, soothing them with his tongue, before dipping inside to once again challenge her tongue to an erotic duel of thrusts and parries.

She needed to be closer to him. Sliding her hands beneath his T-shirt, she reveled in the warmth of his bare skin, delighted in the pounding of his heart beneath her questing palms. Like an explorer on a royal crusade, she made her way up and over every muscular ridge until her fingertips brushed against his male nipples.

Growling deep in this throat, Sam lowered her onto the couch, continuing their kiss but accelerating its intimacy. His weight created an electric contact against her hips. His knee bargained with hers, sliding between her legs and increasing the seductiveness of their embrace. Her body was on fire as she pulled him even closer, arching up into his body to meet the driving urgency.

Sam knew exactly where to touch, where to linger,

when to surge ahead, when to use restraint, how to undermine every last one of her defenses until she was hot and trembling with desire.

Cassie reeled drunkenly in a sensory world where passion ruled and prudence disappeared. His aroused body, his hard lips, and his seductively exploring hands all conveyed a nearly intolerable level of male desire.

His hands slid beneath her T-shirt to cup her breasts as he murmured his delight with her, shifting a string of kisses down her neck, whispering sweetly wicked words into her ear as he brushed his thumbs over the silky material of her bra, finding her nipple and caressing it.

She gasped his name, awed by the powerful surge of pure pleasure that spread through her body and pooled with heated dampness in the deepest recesses. No wonder women found it hard to say no. She'd never experienced anything like this before, never felt this awesome surge of need, of blind yearning. For Sam, only for him.

"The Marines have landed," he whispered seductively, shifting his hands so that he now cupped her breasts. "And are moving in to evaluate the terrain. Mmm, sweet, sweet terrain." He moved her T-shirt out of his way and lowered his head. She shivered with delight at the feel of his warm breath through the thin silky material of her bra. She felt her nipples tingle and stir at his approach.

And then he was there, surrounding her, tugging her into his mouth, driving her even wilder with desire.

Spearing her fingers through his hair, she arched her back and held him even closer, allowing him to work even more magic on her. Seductive magic, man-to-woman magic, that spun a dangerous enchantment.

Then the spell was abruptly broken by the sound of a booming voice. "Hey, I thought I said no making out on the couch."

Chapter Nine

Cassie's startled shriek rang in Sam's ears as she yanked her T-shirt down and hastily shoved him off her, dumping him on the floor. As if that weren't embarrassingly painful enough, Sam cracked his funny bone on the corner of the coffee table on his way down.

"Joe, what did you do?" Prudence demanded from behind her husband.

"Me? Hey, I was just kidding around…"

Prudence put her hand over Joe's mouth. "I'm sorry, you two. We obviously walked in at an embarrassing moment."

"Let me have just one shot at him," Sam growled from the floor. "Just one."

"Stop it, you two!" Prudence's voice reflected her exasperation.

Cassie shook her head and looked as if she wished she were anyplace else on the face of the earth.

The expression on her face increased Sam's anger

on her behalf. He leapt to his feet, slowed slightly by the fact that he'd almost tripped on one of Matt's baby toys.

"Remember, no hitting," Prudence warned Sam, eyeing him warily.

"I think Joe owes Cassie an apology."

"I agree," Prudence said. She gave Joe a warning look before removing her hand from her husband's mouth. "Go ahead, Joe."

"I'm sorry if I embarrassed you, Cassie," Joe said gruffly. "As for you, baby brother—" his voice turned mocking "—what kind of Marine are you to end up on the floor when a little lady gives you a tiny push?"

"The kind that can whip you with one hand tied behind my back," Sam growled.

Rolling her eyes in exasperation, Prudence used her teacher voice. "Stop it, both of you." She placed a hand in the middle of each man's chest. "You're only making the situation worse for Cassie. I apologize for them both." This time Prudence spoke directly to Cassie. "I'm sorry they are such blockheads. But at least now you know the truth. Along with their charming ways and blue eyes, the Wilder men possess a mutant blockhead gene. It makes them do dumb things, especially where the women in their lives are concerned."

Was she the woman in Sam's life? Cassie wondered. And would Prudence be so kind if she knew about Cassie's own background? She knew from the little Sam had said on the way over here that Prudence had been Joe's commanding officer's daughter. That she came from a military background, a very good family. And she knew that Sam also came from a good family, a solid family.

"I can see their behavior has left you momentarily speechless..." Prudence continued.

"I'm never speechless," Cassie said, regaining her composure and her fighting spirit.

"And I wouldn't blame you if you never spoke to Joe again..."

"If Joe gives me any trouble, I'll run the nude photo of him as a baby in the magazine. Right next to the one of Sam."

Both men looked suitably horrified at the possibility.

Prudence just grinned. "I like you, Cassie Jones."

"Thanks. I like you, too."

"It takes a special kind of woman to cope with a Wilder man. But I think you've got what it takes. I think you'll do just fine."

Cassie didn't know about that. How could she do just fine when she'd almost made love with Sam on his brother and sister-in-law's couch? How tacky was that? How out of control?

The incident proved beyond a shadow of a doubt that she wasn't to be trusted where Sam was concerned. He could sneak below her defenses like one of those stealth bombers.

It had all happened so quickly. Sure, she was a woman who was learning to enjoy taking risks now and again, but this was one risk she wasn't prepared to take. She couldn't. There was no future in this, it was a false situation set up by the close proximity she and Sam had been in during the past week.

They'd spent almost every waking moment together. It was only natural that the spark of attraction between them would flare up.

There's nothing natural about his interest in you. It's all surface flash. Fool's gold. Maybe that's how she should describe her hair color instead of whiplash blonde.

Cassie had always been good at presenting a false facade to the world, keeping her inner turmoil hidden away. She'd learned that skill early on, pretending as a child that everything was fine when it wasn't.

She'd been so certain she could do that again. That she could fake a cool nonchalance about Sam even though the hunger for him smoldered deep inside.

Tonight she'd gotten burned. It was a lesson she wouldn't soon forget.

Cassie awoke the next morning with a headache. She needed to get working on writing this story about Sam. The sooner she had the story written, the sooner she could move on. Just as Sam would move on.

Sure, he'd told her in the car last night that she wasn't alone anymore, but he hadn't really meant those words. He'd only said them to be kind.

And she had no doubt that basically Sam was a kind man. She'd seen signs of that when he'd interacted with baby Matt last night.

She also knew he could be warrior-tough when the occasion warranted it. She could still remember the remote look on Sam's face when Al had photographed him the other day, with his so-called battle face on.

The problem was she could remember every tiny thing about Sam—the way the lines at the corners of his eyes crinkled when he smiled, the way he wasn't intimidated by her questions or her challenges, the way he seemed to look at her as if she were an incredible puzzle that he relished figuring out. Maybe he looked at all women that way. The attractive ones, anyway.

To be fair, she had noticed that he was basically polite to any woman who crossed his path, again reacting with an old-fashioned courtesy that was often so lacking in the men Cassie had dated recently. It was as if Sam were a throwback to the age of chivalry and the knights of old.

There she was, back at the fairy-tale imagery again. She remembered Sam telling her at one point that one of the Marine Corps' most successful recruiting ad campaigns had been the one with the Dungeons & Dragons theme, evoking the image of knights of old using their swords to ward off evil.

She could easily picture Sam wearing a suit of armor, fighting for good versus evil. In fact, wearing those black jeans and T-shirt last night he'd looked a bit like a modern-day version of a black knight, a renegade who didn't follow the rules.

She could also easily picture him wearing his workout clothes from the gym, his muscles rippling as he moved. He didn't have a weight lifter's body, he just had a really good body.

Maybe this was all physical attraction. Maybe she was no better than Sam, only attracted to him by his good looks and nothing more. It was only hormones, powerful to be sure, but no danger to her heart.

If only.

She knew that wasn't the case. Knew it with her deepest soul. Yes, she was physically attracted to Sam, but there was so much more to it than that. He touched her heart with his warm smiles, his coaxing grins, his Tigger impersonation. He met her challenges and spurred her on.

She'd been so careful not to have her plans derailed by blind passion. She'd been so focused on her career as a journalist.

She glanced down at the tiny heart tattoo near her wrist. Never wear your heart on your sleeve. She'd gotten the tattoo after her mother's funeral. Cassie had been the only one there, along with a minister provided by the funeral home. The minister had never met her mother. They'd only recently moved again, to Toledo this time, so there hadn't been time to meet people.

There hadn't been time, period. Not for her mother, who had combined too many powerful over-the-counter cold pills with too much alcohol. Cassie wanted to believe that her mother hadn't done it deliberately, hadn't committed suicide. But the truth was she didn't know. She'd never really know, not for sure.

The police had told her at the time that the number of pills suggested that the death was accidental and that's how they ruled it. But Cassie had never known and that ate away at her, bit by bit, undermining her confidence, sliding the emotional rug out from under her at the most unexpected moments.

Which was why she was glad she had the tattoo to remind her. Never wear your heart on your sleeve. You had to be tough to survive. Loving a man too much could do you in—emotionally and physically. You had to be self-sufficient first and foremost.

And so she'd built walls around herself. Sam was right about that. She had grown thorns to keep others at bay. But he'd cut right through them, steadfastly making his way to her heart.

Just because she didn't wear her heart on her sleeve didn't mean she didn't have a heart. She did. A heart that was at risk of belonging to Sam.

Cassie wasn't coming. He'd scared her off. Sam heaped silent curses on his wayward older brother for walking in on them last night.

Sam had waited out on the track field for an extra ten minutes and had ended up forgoing his usual run to check the gym to see if she'd gone there, thinking to find him there instead. She hadn't.

He could call her, she'd given him her cell phone number early on. But first he'd have to figure out what to say to her. And frankly, he didn't have a clue. Clearly it was time to review his battle plan here, time to quickly go over the decision cycle every Marine Corps officer went through—observation, orientation, decision and action.

He'd observed that Cassie was an incredible woman. He'd oriented himself into a position to spend a lot of time with her. His decision was that he clearly wanted her more than he'd wanted any other woman in his entire life. His course of action, to make love to her.

So why wasn't it that easy? Because Cassie was a complicated woman. He'd known that the first time he'd seen her. And known that there was more to her than the Tough Chick exterior she hoped to project. He'd always sensed an inner vulnerability in her.

Knowing that, how could he coldheartedly plan her seduction based on the premises of fighting a war? What kind of relationship did he foresee with Cassie?

Last night he'd pictured her holding his baby on her lap. That sounded pretty darn serious to him. Where *was* this relationship going?

Jeez, these were girl questions. They'd certainly never arisen with him before. He'd never wondered where a relationship with a woman was going. He pretty much knew—having a good time together while it lasted.

But Cassie was different. He'd never had to chase after a woman before, never had to struggle to try to figure out what she was thinking or feeling.

He remembered a few girlfriends in his past accusing him of hiding his emotions. But that's what guys did. Women weren't supposed to do that. They weren't supposed to make things this hard to figure out.

Sam's inability to appraise the situation irked him. He'd been so sure that reviewing his four-step mental process—observation, orientation, decision and action—would do the trick.

It worked great with military encounters.

Which was probably the problem. He'd been trained to react with hair-trigger quickness to all kinds of situations. He'd had to depend on that training in life-threatening conditions.

But this was not a military encounter. This was a personal encounter, an intensely personal one at that. And it was disconcerting to realize he didn't have a clue as to how to react in this situation.

Sam only knew one thing for sure, next time he saw his brother Joe, he was going to wipe the floor with him.

"You're here."

Cassie was surprised at the relief in Sam's voice. "Yes, I'm here. In body if not in spirit," she added in a muttered undertone. The headache she'd woken up with had intensified to gigantic proportions.

She was sitting next to Sam's desk, working on her laptop. Her deadline was fast approaching.

"Are you okay?"

"I'm fine," she said coolly. "I just need to concentrate on getting this feature done."

Sam tried telling himself that she wasn't really telling him he was merely a feature story and nothing more to her. Then he gave himself permission to drink in the very sight of her. She was wearing a black sleeveless knit top that clung to her breasts. The turtleneck collar gave the appearance that this was not a sexy piece of clothing, but that was clearly not the case. The slacks she wore were beige with little black lines on them.

All in all, her appearance was more professional and less colorful than it had been in the past. Which made him wonder why she was dressed this way. Was she already planning ahead, ready to move on to the next story?

He saw the tiny heart tattoo as she shifted her wrist while typing. And was reassured by its presence. She was still Cassie, fiery and unpredictable. Sexy and irresistible.

Still, she looked pale and tired. He wondered if she'd tossed and turned last night the way he had. He'd never planned for things to get out of hand the way they had last night. He felt guilty at the possibility that he was to blame for her exhaustion.

He tried to make it up to her. "Would you like to work here at my desk? I've got to go give presentations to several officer training classes today, so you're welcome to stay and use my desk.''

"Is your presentation classified or something?''

"No.''

"Then I'll come with you.''

She needed to see him interacting with more Marines. But it was hard concentrating, due to her headache and due to the fact that Sam had almost made love to her last night.

Cassie deliberately focused on his speaking style and the reaction of the Marines in the classroom. They clearly viewed him with respect and listened to what he told them about the stress of decision-making in life-and-death situations, about the need for a cool head.

Her own head was anything but cool. By the time four o'clock rolled around Cassie knew she couldn't take it any longer. The migraine she was fighting had won, hands down. She reluctantly had to concede defeat.

"That's the last class for today,'' Sam said. "I thought you might have raised your hand to ask a few questions.''

"No.'' She had taken note of his comment when someone had asked about him joining as an enlisted man. He'd talked about coming from a long tradition of enlisted men, and how he and his brothers had teased Mark when he'd become an officer. Mark reminded him of that now that Sam had become an officer himself.

Those were the last notes she'd taken. Since then it had taken all her energy just to stay upright. She didn't get many of these headaches, but when they came they were debilitating.

"You okay?" Sam asked in concern as she swayed slightly.

"I've got a migraine." Her voice was a husky whisper.

"Do you have medication you take for it?"

"Not with me."

He quickly led her to his office chair and sat her down. "My mom got migraines when we were stationed down South, something about the humidity seemed to trigger them. Which works best for you, hot or cold compress?"

"Hot."

"Stay here a second." Waving someone over, he requested a paper towel dipped in warm water.

"No," Cassie said sharply. She couldn't stand the thought of anyone seeing her while she was ill, of watching her with pity while she sat there with a compress on her forehead like an invalid. It reminded her of the many times she'd placed a cold compress on her mother's forehead when she was suffering from a terrible hangover. "I just need to go home."

"Why don't you let me drive you."

She couldn't nod, it hurt too much. Much as she hated to admit it, she was in no shape to drive. "Okay."

Sam knew she had to be in bad shape for her to agree to let him drive her red Miata. She treated that car like a favored pet. He remembered the first day they'd met, when she'd warned him not to leave fingerprints on her dash. She was so full of fire and life. But not at the moment. Now she was as pale as a waif as he put his arm around her and led her outside, asking where her car was parked.

He located it without too much difficulty; after all,

he'd located drop points from two miles up. He tried to make her as comfortable as possible, adjusting the passenger seat so that she was almost reclining, not making any abrupt turns or sudden stops.

They reached her apartment, which was clear on the other side of Washington, D.C. in record time and once again he was lucky enough to find a parking space near the front door. The fact that it was midafternoon and most people were still at work no doubt helped ease the parking situation.

Sam helped Cassie inside, waiting for her to wave him away and send him packing. She didn't. She was practically swaying on her feet. Afraid she'd fall, he kept his arm firmly around her as they entered the elevator. Mrs. Friedman was already inside.

"Why, hello, you two." The older woman gave them an avidly curious look. "So nice to see you both again."

Cassie just kept her eyes closed, the bright light in the elevator proving to be too much for her.

"Is something wrong, Cassandra?" Mrs. Friedman asked. "You don't seem like yourself."

"She has a terrible migraine," Sam answered on her behalf.

"Oh, you poor dear. My Saul gets those sometimes. You just lie down and take things easy, you hear?"

Cassie winced. With Mrs. Friedman's piercing voice it was hard not to hear. And sound, like light, made her head pound even more.

Which was why she was so grateful when the elevator doors opened and Sam escorted her out. She couldn't get the key into her lock so Sam took it from her. Seconds later he had her inside.

"Couch or bed?" he asked.

"Bed," she whispered.

Sam escorted her into her bedroom, keeping his arm around her. This wasn't the way he'd imagined his first visit to her bedroom would take place. He'd fantasized about taking her to bed, about slowly peeling her Tough Chick T-shirt off, of unfastening her bra, of discovering the softness of her bare breasts. Now he felt guilty for even thinking such things.

Sitting her on the bed, he knelt and removed her shoes. Then he moved some of the pillows aside so she could lie down on top of the soft comforter. It must be feathers, because she sank onto it. He carefully placed a small blanket over her. "Where's your medicine?"

"Top shelf, bathroom medicine cabinet."

If he thought there was something intimate about going into her bedroom, pawing through her medicine cabinet was even more intimidating. He quickly overlooked feminine products and pulled down the prescription medication. He brought her a glass of cold water to take it with and a warmed washcloth for a hot compress for her head.

After she'd taken her medication he sat on the far side of the bed to wait.

"You don't have to stay."

"I'm not leaving you alone. Try to get some sleep. I'll be right here if you need anything."

She was quiet for a while, as if she lacked even the energy to talk. Sam automatically studied his surroundings, his training as a Marine such that he always noted exits first. But he looked beyond that. The room was bright and colorful, yet soft and sensual. Red was clearly her favorite color.

He already knew her favorite movie was *Back to*

the Future. An odd choice he'd thought when she'd first told him. But her voice had been almost wistful when she'd talked about Michael J. Fox's character going back in time and changing the man his father had become. He'd wondered if she'd wished she could have changed things for her own mother that way.

"I hate having people see me when I'm sick," she suddenly said, her voice unsteady.

"Shh." He placed a soothing hand on her forehead, replacing the compress with his own comforting touch. "I'm not people."

"No," she whispered, clearly groggy from the strong medication. "You're Sam. Too-good-to-be-true Sam."

"I'm not too good to be true, Cassie."

But she'd already drifted off to sleep and couldn't hear him.

Chapter Ten

Cassie woke the next morning thinking she'd had the strangest dreams. They had to be dreams. Caused by the medication, perhaps? Sam couldn't have spent the night with her, crawling beneath the fluffy duvet with her.

Panicked, she lifted the covers to find she was no longer wearing the same clothes she'd had on yesterday. Instead she was wearing her only pair of flannel pajamas.

Which didn't mean anything. She'd probably removed her clothes herself during a midnight trip to the bathroom.

Now that she was awake, images were coming back to her. Images of Sam. Sitting her up and gently peeling her constrictive turtleneck top off, replacing it with the softness of a button-down flannel pajama top. It *hadn't* been a dream.

The note on her bedside table confirmed that. Sam had left it for her. She read it with some trepidation.

Exactly what had happened last night? Was there more, something she didn't remember? She was still wearing her bra. Which meant what?

Dear Cassie,
Sorry I had to leave this morning but when I woke you at six you seemed better.

He'd woken her at six? What time was it now? She checked her brushed-stainless-steel alarm clock. Well after ten.
She continued reading.

So I headed back to the base. I'll call you at noon. Don't leave this bed until then, that's an order. You need the rest. I fear I've tired you out.

Tired her out? How? When? What *had* they been doing last night? She knew the migraine medication knocked her out, but surely they hadn't done anything last night...
She picked up the phone and called Sam.
"Captain Wilder." His words were military crisp.
"It's Cassie."
"How are you feeling?" His voice softened.
"Better. What exactly happened last night?"
"You were pretty out of it once you took that pain medicine."
"And?"
"And what?"
"And I went to bed wearing one thing and woke up wearing something else."
"Oh, the pajamas."

"Yes. Among other things. Did I say or do anything last night that I shouldn't have?"

"Like what?"

"Let me put it another way. Did *you* say or do anything last night that *you* shouldn't have."

"Like make love to you, you mean?"

"Yes."

"Trust me, when I make love to you, you'll know it."

"So we didn't…?"

"No, we didn't. I did change your clothes because you were clearly uncomfortable and in no shape to do it yourself. I like the pajamas with the red hearts." His voice turned rough and husky. "But I liked the little red silk number even better."

"You pawed through my nightgowns?"

"Hey, you don't have to make me sound like some kind of pervert or something. I was only trying to help."

"I'll bet."

"I kept my eyes closed the whole time."

"And if I believe that, you've got land in Arizona to sell me, right?"

He laughed. "Okay, so I only kept them closed part of the time."

More images were coming back to her now, more comforting images of him soothing her pain, of him taking care of her. She'd never had anyone take care of her before. She didn't know what to say, how to react.

"Hey, are you still there?" Sam said.

"Yes."

"You're not angry, are you?"

"About what?"

"About my staying with you."

"No, I'm not angry."

"Good. Take it easy today and I'll bring you some Szechuan Chinese tonight. Kung Pao chicken and Mongolian beef, okay? Or would that be too much for you?"

"Bring it on, Captain Wilder." Pure bravado on her part and not a word of truth. Reality was that this…this thing between her and Sam…was all too much for her. "I can take whatever you dish out."

"I know you can. It's one of the things I love about you."

"Wha-at? What did you say?"

"I said it's one of the things I like about you. See you tonight."

Sam stared at the phone long after he'd hung up. He couldn't believe he'd just used the L word with Cassie. She'd sounded freaked.

He had to go slow here, he couldn't rush her. Winning her was too important to mess up. He had to do this right. Because this might well turn out to be the most important mission of his life.

Cassie couldn't believe how the rest of the week flew by. Sam's staying the night to take care of her had marked a pivotal point in their relationship. There was no use denying that she'd already fallen for him. It was too late to save herself.

She was trying not to think about things too much, trying to live in the moment and to turn off the inner fears warning her that this wasn't real.

She was relieved that Sam seemed determined to take things slower. They went out to a movie one night, watched a Thursday night football game another. And scattered in between were his Marine duties, an appearance at an ROTC function, a speech at an area middle school.

Friday night brought another formal event, this time something to do with the Armed Services Committee. Sam insisted she wear her burgundy dress again, a fashion no-no. Luckily she'd had it dry cleaned earlier in the week.

Even so, she informed him, "You're never supposed to wear the same formal dress two weeks in a row. People will think I don't own any other formal dresses, which happens to be true but still…"

"I don't care what people think," he murmured. "I only care about you."

How was she supposed to resist him when he said things like that to her? And how was she supposed to resist when he took her in his arms later that night to kiss her?

He'd kissed her several times during the course of the week, but they'd been controlled kisses. She suspected he'd intended for this kiss to be the same. But things quickly escalated in the darkness of his car.

He cupped his hands against her face as he devoured her mouth with his sensual kisses. It wasn't enough. They both wanted more.

Sam trailed his kisses down her throat, licking and nibbling his way along the black silk ribbon artfully tied around her neck. Then he moved on to her bare shoulders while caressing her with a lover's hand.

A second later a sharp crack was followed by his muffled curse as he pulled away from her.

"What is it? What's wrong?" Her voice was husky, her lips still throbbing from his kisses.

"I rammed my elbow against the steering wheel

and hit my funny bone. I'm getting too old to make out in a car,'' he rumbled.

Cassie knew he wanted her to invite him up to her place, but she couldn't. She wasn't ready yet. If he came up, they'd end up making love. She had no doubt about that. But she still had doubts about many other things. For the past few days she'd been trying to ignore them, to just go with the flow, to take this risk of seeing where their relationship would take them.

To bed. That's where he wanted the relationship to go. And so did she. But she wanted more than that. More than just sex. She wanted…a future. With him.

Saturday morning Sam was scheduled to play his biweekly game of basketball with his brother Joe. Cassie was not joining them. She said she had work to do but Sam wasn't fooled; he knew she didn't want to run into his brother again after he'd walked in on them.

He was still ticked off at Joe over that situation.

Consequently their friendly game turned into a no-holds-barred battle.

It didn't help matters any that Joe acted as his own sports announcer, shouting his plays. ''Joe Wilder hits another one from downtown.''

''Joe Wilder is an idiot,'' Sam growled, stealing the ball and shooting a three-pointer.

''This isn't about basketball, this is about a woman.'' Joe shot another basket. ''Cassie. She's gotten to you.''

''What's between Cassie and me is none of your business.'' Sam lunged right, left, then made the jump shot.

"Fine by me." Joe wiped sweat from his eyes and hit another basket.

"Good." Sam took possession of the ball.

"But there's no way I can avoid what's going on between you two when it's going on in my own living room."

Joe ducked as Sam threw the ball at him. "Hey, that was uncalled for."

"I'll tell you what was uncalled for." Sam advanced on him. "You embarrassing her that way."

Joe stood his ground. "I already apologized to her about that."

"Not good enough."

They were about to come to blows when Sam's cell phone rang. Thinking it might be Cassie, he answered it.

It was his mom.

"Prudence told me that you're playing a game of basketball with Joe, is that right?"

"Yes."

"I remember when the two of you would play hoops in our driveway," she recalled fondly, "whichever base our driveway happened to be on at the time. You both hated to lose, so those games were always competitive."

"They still are."

"I'm calling because I have great news. Mark and Vanessa are going to have a baby."

"That's nice." His attention remained on Joe, visually informing him that the matter between them was not over yet.

"Nice?" she repeated in disbelief. "Didn't you hear what I just said?"

"I heard you."

His mom sighed. "You're not still mad at your brother, are you?"

Sam frowned. "Mad at Mark? Why would I be mad at him?"

"I'm talking about Joe."

Sam could tell by the tone of her voice that she knew what was going on. He also knew that his brother hadn't told her anything. Which could only mean one thing.

Covering the receiver, Sam growled at Joe. "Your wife's been talking to our mom."

"Hey, don't blame me. I long ago gave up trying to control what my wife says or does."

"I understand a female reporter has been following you around, doing a story on you," his mother said. "I also understand she's apparently more than just a reporter as far as you're concerned."

"Here, you started this, you talk to Mom." Sam handed the phone to Joe.

"Hi, Mom," Joe said. "Sam? He's fine. Just bowled over by a woman."

Sam quickly realized his tactical error and grabbed the phone back.

"So when are we going to meet this girl?" his mother asked.

"I have no idea. Listen, Mom, I've got to go. I'll call you back later."

He disconnected and glared at his brother. "You think this is all very funny, don't you?"

Joe nodded.

"But then you've always had a twisted sense of humor," Sam added.

"No argument there," Joe agreed with a grin. "So

much for you being the last Wilder bachelor. I'd say your single days were definitely numbered."

"And I'd say it's none of your business. By the way, Mom called to say that Mark and Vanessa are going to have a baby."

"Copycats," Joe said in a grumpy voice. "I can't do anything without my brothers copying my act."

His comment created an opening Sam couldn't resist. "Do you think we're too competitive as brothers?"

"Hey, there's no such thing as *too* competitive."

"It's no piece of cake following in your footsteps all the time. You even stole the nickname Flyboy when we were kids. And you're not even a pilot." Jeez, he sounded like a whiny kid.

"I used to think I'd be a pilot someday. Instead you're the pilot in the family."

The words that had been on Sam's mind for days abruptly came out. "Do you think things have come too easily for me? That I take the easy way out?"

"Of course you do," Joe replied. "So what else is new?"

What was new was the gut-churning turmoil Sam experienced over his brother's words.

Before Cassie knew it—before she was ready for it—her deadline was upon her. She spent all of Saturday working on the story, but it was difficult finding just the right tone. That was nothing new. During the past two weeks she'd started the story about two dozen different ways and hadn't been happy with any of them.

She'd never had a story give her such a hard time.

But then she'd never gone and fallen in love with the subject of one of her stories before.

At the moment Cassie was taking a little break from writing her article to do some math. She and Sam had spent more than one hundred and forty hours together. If a regular evening date consisted of four or five hours, that would mean twenty or twenty-five dates.

Which meant that even though she and Sam had actually known each other for two weeks, they had spent as much time together as couples who had gone together much longer.

Okay, she knew she was grasping at straws here. But for some reason she'd been feeling out of sorts all day. Maybe it was her looming deadline and the stress that brought with it. Or maybe it was the realization that this story was quickly coming to an end and she had no idea where she and Sam would be going from here.

Actually, Sam was on his way over at this very minute. He'd called on his cell phone, sounding a bit strange, saying he needed to talk to her. He'd hung up before she could ask him for more information.

And so here she was, counting the hours she'd known him like one of those fairy-tale misers hoarding their gold.

She could sense the hyper vibes coming off Sam the moment she let him into her apartment a few minutes later. Instead of settling on her comfy red couch as he usually did, he started pacing.

For the first moment or two she merely enjoying watching him. His well-worn jeans conformed to his lower body, while his black U.S.M.C. T-shirt fit him like a glove as it always did. She loved that T-shirt.

She remembered sliding her fingers beneath it when they'd made out on his brother's couch.

The memory made her hot and flustered, and further increased her already nervous state.

"What's up?" she asked, trying to sound bright and perky instead of tense and scared.

No answer. Just more pacing.

This must be some kind of male thing. Last she'd heard, Sam and his brother were going to play a one-on-one game of basketball today. Was that what had gotten him all riled up?

"Did you lose the basketball game to your brother?" She knew how competitive Marines were. And when the Marines were brothers, that probably upped the ante.

"No, I did not lose!" He sounded furious that she'd even considered that a possibility.

His irritation took her aback. "Okay, then." She took a deep breath. "What did you want to talk about?"

"Don't rush me."

Okay, now she was getting aggravated. "Listen, you're the one who called me."

"I know, I know. I just don't want to be rushed, okay?"

"Okay, fine. You go ahead and keep pacing. I've got work to do." She sat on the couch, then leaned forward to type on her laptop perched on the painted red pine bench that served as her coffee table.

Sam knew he was being a jerk but he couldn't seem to help himself. He had the same pit-of-his-stomach feeling that he'd had when that plane's engine had malfunctioned.

He vividly remembered Cassie saying to him once,

"It must be nice to have your life all laid out for you. No need to make decisions on your own, no need to make sacrifices. It was easy for you to follow in your family's footsteps by becoming a Marine. I suspect a lot of things have come easily for you, Sam."

Maybe they had in the past but it didn't feel that way now. Now it felt as if he was shoving boulders uphill. Which wouldn't have been a big deal had it been a physical challenge he was dealing with. But this internal stuff drove him nuts. He didn't like second-guessing all his life decisions and that's what he'd been doing.

After his brush with death in that emergency landing, Sam had wondered about a lot of things: wondered what it was he really wanted out of life; wondered if he'd only chosen the Marine Corps because it was the easy thing to do; wondered what his life would have been like had he made other choices.

While Sam relished challenges, he didn't like this uncertainty he was experiencing. He didn't even know how to handle things with Cassie.

He was a man accustomed to devising a plan and making it work. He wasn't used to inner turmoil. Not that he hadn't experienced it during his lifetime, but he'd learned to stomp it out. Uncertainty had no place on a battlefield or in the cockpit. That was a sure way to get you and those under your command killed.

Sam wanted to talk to Cassie about all this stuff, which was why he'd called her, but then he'd realized that he couldn't do that. He knew that as a representative of the Marine Corps he couldn't show her his doubts about becoming a Marine and staying in the Corps, they could end up in her story. He felt disloyal even considering such topics.

Maybe all this stupid soul-searching stuff was just frustration at being grounded, at being stuck at Quantico. Maybe that's why Joe's comment had struck him as deeply as it had. Because he was already raw.

Cassie knew something was up, knew Sam was seething with some kind of emotions. But she was done playing twenty questions with him. His curt *Don't rush me* had definitely hit her the wrong way, because it's what her mom used to say when Cassie had tried to get her to do something she didn't want to do.

She tried to concentrate on her article, but it was impossible with him there.

Maybe he was trying to come up with the words to break things off with her. Maybe he'd grown tired of the chase and was ready to move on.

"Look, if you're not going to talk to me, then at least sit down someplace instead of prowling around like a caged tiger."

He gave her a disgruntled glare but did sit down.

She stayed quiet another few minutes. Then she just couldn't take it anymore. "Are you here to call it quits?"

Her abrupt question clearly startled him. "No."

"Then tell me what's the matter."

"Nothing is the matter."

She knew darn well that was a lie. "You said you wanted to talk to me. So talk to me. Please."

"I changed my mind."

Okay, now she was getting angry. "I've talked to you about things I haven't talked to with anyone. Do you think it was easy for me to reveal my background to you, to talk about my past and open up that way? It wasn't easy. It was damn hard. But I did it. And now here you are, refusing to reciprocate in even the smallest way by telling me what's got you so upset.''

"I'm not a journalist who'll print your confession for millions to read," Sam angrily pointed out.

"If you tell me to keep something off the record, I'll do that. I won't put it in the article without your permission."

But Sam hesitated, his blue eyes guarded.

And Cassie retreated, stung by what she perceived to be his refusal to trust her.

"Are you only interested in me because of the story you're doing?" Sam abruptly demanded.

How dare he come in here and demand to know how she felt, when he didn't say a word about his own emotions and when he clearly didn't trust her not to betray him.

Cassie turned the tables on him by asking, "What about you? Why are you interested in me? Where do you see this thing between us going? Do you see a future for it? For us? Because I don't want to be one of a bevy of women in your life. You, the man reputed to have the Teflon heart." Almost shaking now with pent-up emotion, she reached out and grabbed a framed photograph. "Here." She thrust it at him. "What do you think of her?"

"There's no way I'd be interested in her," Sam said adamantly.

That's what she'd been afraid of all along. Because the photograph she'd just shown him was one taken of her before her transformation.

His rejection was a tangible thing, bruising her as surely as a slap. Pain rammed into her, taking her breath away. Her worst fear had just come true. Sam had immediately dismissed the "real" Cassie without all the blond trappings.

She felt the sting of tears in her eyes and knew she had to get him out of her apartment. When emotionally threatened in the past, she'd always battened down the hatches and pulled up the drawbridge. All she had left was her pride. She would *not* let him see her cry. That was not an option. Which meant he had to go—now. Right now. "I think you should leave."

"Why?"

"Just go!"

"Not until you tell me what this is all about." Sam used his military command voice.

"Sure, now you want to talk," she retorted. "Five seconds ago you told me to butt out."

"Is that what this is about…?"

He reached for her, she sidestepped him and he instead knocked over a pile of papers from the bench coffee table.

"Don't read that," she told him.

But it was already too late. The damage had been done.

She remembered when she'd written that draft, that very first night when she'd still been aggravated with him and his cocky attitude.

She watched his eyes turn cold as he read her opening line. "Marine Corps poster boy of the month, Captain Sam Wilder, may look like a hero, but it takes more than good looks to be truly heroic. Something is lacking here…"

"Something's lacking, huh?" Rigid with anger, Sam dropped the paper back on the table. "You're the one who's lacking something. Honor." He stormed out before she had the chance to say a word in her own defense, leaving her alone once again.

Chapter Eleven

After Sam's departure, Cassie finally allowed the scalding tears to fall freely. He hadn't given her the chance to explain that she'd changed the story since then.

But did it really matter? The damage had already been done when she'd handed him that photo of her and he'd said what he had. What did one more nail in the coffin of their relationship matter?

The pain came in recurring waves of burning tears followed by periods of numbness. She was awash in painful emotions as her feelings of inferiority returned tenfold. Cassie had been playing a role of a confident woman, but inside she'd continued to be the imposter who was hiding her inner self, the self that whispered she'd never be good enough for someone to love.

Maybe Sam was right. Maybe she did lack honor. Maybe it was dishonorable of her to pretend to be something she wasn't. She didn't know anymore. She only knew that she hadn't hurt this much since her mother's death.

Glancing down, she traced the tiny heart tattoo near her wrist with fingers that trembled. She'd known she was playing with fire, known that loving Sam would leave her vulnerable. She should have kept her defenses up, should have known that fairy tales weren't real.

But Sam had had the ability to touch her as no other. From their first kiss to their last, he'd made her see stars and fireworks. He'd made her heart thrill to the magic of his embrace. He'd made her start to believe that maybe, just maybe, happily-ever-afters didn't just occur in fairy tales.

But then reality had come crashing in on her little fantasy world. And with it had come the knowledge that Sam had never said he loved her, other than that one time when he'd used the word kiddingly. *That's one of the things I love about you,* he'd told her over the phone.

It was a throwaway comment, one people used with one another. It didn't mean anything.

She remembered how confident she'd been when she'd first walked into Quantico. Payback time had come for Sam Wilder and his cocky arrogance. Looking back now, she wondered what on earth had made her think she was the woman to teach him a lesson.

Instead, Cassie was the one who'd learned a painful truth. She'd been playing a dangerous game disguising her real self. She'd known it yet hadn't been able to stop herself from doing it. Like a nightmare where you saw the train heading right at you but were frozen in place, unable to move away.

Her worst nightmare had come true. Sam had seen

the "real" her and confirmed that there was no way he'd be interested in her.

It was a good thing she'd found that out before they'd made love. That should prove some consolation. But it didn't.

Because the bottom line here was that she'd fallen in love with a man who could never love the real her.

After a sleepless night, Cassie returned to work the next morning. The magazine headquarters almost seemed like an alien place to her now, after spending so much time with Sam down in Quantico. The regular receptionist, Andrea, greeted her warmly before buzzing her through.

The place was filled with the sounds of people— talking on phones, typing on keyboards blended with the whir of printers spitting out what they'd written. Her editor Phil was in his glassed-in corner office, the door open, the blinds shut. All was well in the magazine's world.

But all was not well in Cassie's world.

She thought she'd hidden that fact beneath the makeup she'd meticulous applied, as she did every morning since her make-over. But Al saw through her attempts when he stopped by her desk later that morning.

"Everything okay?"

"Absolutely," she lied.

"No offense, but you don't look so good."

"I must be coming down with a bug."

"Yeah, I saw signs of that when I took that photo of you and Sam. Too bad there's no inoculation against this kind of thing."

"Yeah, I know what you mean." Cassie would have thought her mother's experiences would have made her immune to the pitfalls of love. While that had always prevented her from getting derailed in the past, it hadn't worked with Sam.

"Listen, if something happened between you and Sam that you need to talk about, you could try talking to me." Al fiddled with the camera around his neck instead of looking at her. "I don't know how good I'd be at giving you advice, but you're welcome to try if you feel you have to."

She was deeply touched by his awkward offer of moral support. "That's not necessary, but thanks. It's my own fault. I stupidly started believing in fairy tales." She looked down at the book open on her desk. "You know what you find when you look up fairy tale in the thesaurus, Al?"

He shook his head.

"Lies. You'll find it's listed under lies."

Sam discovered that the first day without Cassie was bad. The second day was worse. And the third day was really the pits. That's when Striker stopped by and took Sam out for a little liquid refreshment after work.

The bar they stopped at was one relatively near the base, but not so close that they'd run into too many people they knew. The large-screen TV reminded Sam of the sports bar where he and Cassie had watched the football game.

That had happened a lot lately: things reminding him of Cassie. The running track, the weight room, the empty chair beside his desk. They all triggered vivid memories of her.

His chest tightened as if gripped in a vise.

"How could I have been so mistaken, thinking she

had real feelings for me? It was all a con. You want to hear the funny thing?'' Sam took a swallow of cold beer. ''I was in love with her. I planned on telling her that last night before everything got messed up.'' He studied the Mexican beer label on the bottle. It, too, reminded him of Cassie and the night they'd eaten Mexican dinner together and she'd stolen half his ice-cream dessert. The woman had ended up stealing much more than just dessert.

''It stinks,'' Striker agreed.

''I thought I could be her knight in shining armor,'' Sam noted bitterly. ''How stupid is that?''

''You know, I've faced armed conflicts without elevating my heart rate. But love?'' Striker shook his head. ''Man, that's something bound to scare you spitless.''

''No kidding.'' Sam took another swallow of his beer. ''Women. Who can figure them out? And Cassie, she's even worse than most. She's totally indecipherable. The best code crackers could have a tough time with her.''

''She's not the only female on the planet,'' Striker said. ''There are plenty of other women out there. In fact, there are several right here in this bar who have been giving you the eye. Like that blonde over there—''

''I'm off blondes,'' Sam interrupted him.

''Okay, then how about that brunette?''

''What brunette?''

''The one with the bare midriff. I'm sure she'd be more than glad to help cheer you up.''

Sam just shook his head, not even bothering to look. ''Forget it. I'm not interested. Cassie has ruined me for any other woman.''

"Bummer." Striker ordered another round of beers. "You never did say exactly what happened with you two."

"I read what she'd written about me for her article. You know she'd been following me around for two weeks, you'd think she'd get it right."

"So it was something she wrote?"

Sam nodded broodingly.

"Did she insult the Marine Corps?"

"She insulted me. Something about it taking more than good looks to be truly heroic." Sam said the words in an offhand manner, as if they hadn't been burned into his memory banks. "How something was lacking…"

"Ouch." Striker winced. "Talk about going for the jugular."

"Tell me about it. And it didn't help matters any that only a few hours before that my brother Joe was telling me that I always take the easy way out, that things have come too easily for me."

"Not true. You might make it look like that, but there's nothing easy about becoming an aviator in the United States Marine Corps. There's nothing easy about the Corps, period. Pain is just weakness leaving the body. That's what Marines believe."

Which explained why Sam had been feeling so rotten lately. Pain was just the memory of Cassie leaving his body and mind. But she wasn't leaving, she stubbornly stayed put no matter how hard he tried to evict her.

Maybe there was a reason for that. Maybe there was still unfinished business between them. "I don't get why she wrote what she did."

"Did you ask her?"

"No, I stormed out of there as if my boots were on fire."

"A logical move."

"Maybe. But I've still got a long list of unanswered questions. She might wear a Tough Chick T-shirt, but she's not really the kind of woman to lead a man on. The chemistry between us was real and more powerful than an F-17."

"An F-17, huh? That's a powerful chunk of aeronautic design."

"I know."

"Maybe you're just missing flying, you ever consider that? Maybe that's what's got you all messed up."

"I wish it was that easy, but it's not. Sure I miss flying, but I know I'll be back soon. My temporary assignment here is almost done."

"That should make you feel better."

"Yeah, it should, but it doesn't." The more they talked, the more Sam realized he couldn't leave things the way they were. He had to talk to Cassie.

There were too many questions in his own mind. He needed to find out why she'd written the things she had. He'd left too many things unsaid. They needed to have it all out, lay their cards on the table and have the chips fall where they may.

He wasn't going to give up on her yet; he wasn't going to let her get away without a fight. It may have taken him three long days to reach that decision but he'd reached it now and he planned on taking immediate action.

"I have to talk to Cassie."

Striker blinked at him. "What?"

"I have to go talk to Cassie." Sam leapt to his feet.

"Right now?"

"Yes, right now." Sam gave him a handful of bills. "The drinks are on me."

In his hurry to exit the crowded bar, Sam bumped into someone near the door. "Sorry," he said automatically before realizing he knew the guy. It was Al, Cassie's photographer friend. "What are you doing here?" Sam demanded. "Did Cassie send you?" Maybe she'd reached the same conclusion Sam had, that they needed to talk.

"No, she did not send me." Al glared at him. "I was doing a photo shoot in the area and decided to stop off for a drink afterward. I had no idea you'd be here. I would have thought you'd pick up chicks in one of those dives closer to the base."

"I am not here to pick up chicks."

"Sure. Whatever." Al didn't look as though he believed a word Sam said. "I just wish that Cassie had never gone to that stupid press conference of yours in the first place."

This was the first time Sam had heard that Cassie had been there that day.

"Wait a minute. Are you talking about the press conference when I first returned to the States after the incident?" Al made no reply but Sam knew that had to be the case. He hadn't done any other press conferences. Other press, yes, but not like that.

"I don't have anything else to say," Al declared.

Sam knew how to get answers when he wanted them, and he used every single thing he'd learned in psychological operations training to push Al's buttons and get into his head. He also used his considerable presence and sheer bulk along with a voice accustomed to getting men to follow orders. "You better talk to me, and you better talk to me *now*. Because I'll warn you, you do not want to tee off an impatient Marine.'' Sam let his body language do the rest of the talking. In the end, he overcame Al's resistance in short order.

Al revealed what Sam wanted to know and ended by concluding, ''I'm only telling you this because I care about the kid. Otherwise none of your military mayhem maneuvers would have worked on me,'' Al said proudly.

Sam just shook his head, still amazed at what Al had disclosed. ''She changed her appearance after my press conference? Because I didn't call on her?''

''Because she was tired of being overlooked. She wanted to become a whiplash blonde, and she did.''

Sam had even more questions for Cassie now. But first he had to find her. The minute he was in his car, he called her, but she didn't answer her phone at home or at work.

It was almost eight, she should be home by now. Unless she was out on a date? His cell phone went dead.

Muttering under his breath, he headed to a coffee place across the street and used their payphone. Again no answer. Ordering a large black coffee to go, he was absently looking at the racks near the counter when he saw his name on the cover of *Capital Magazine*. The new issue had come out.

He wasn't sure what made him buy a copy, masochism maybe. He tossed the magazine into his car and headed for her apartment. The doorman told him that she hadn't come in yet.

So Sam waited in his car with his coffee and the magazine. He opened it and started reading. But that dreaded opening line was no longer there. Unlike the previous draft he'd seen, this time she'd written of her admiration for him and for all those who were willing to give their lives for their country, to fight for everyone's freedom. He could also see that she was a very talented writer with a brilliant future ahead of her.

He'd never thought of her that way before. Sure, he'd figured she must be pretty good at what she did, but he'd never pursued the thought beyond that point. Now he realized how very good she was and he experienced a momentary doubt.

Her byline listed her as Cassandra Jones. An impressive-looking name. He ran his finger over the print. She was an up-and-coming talent. Maybe a Marine like him didn't have much to offer her, after all.

Then he remembered when Cassie had told him about her childhood and about always having to look out for herself, about having no one but herself to depend upon. Sam wanted her to depend on *him*. He wanted to fight her battles, wanted to win her heart.

So caught up was he in his own thoughts that he almost missed seeing her as she made her way toward her apartment building. With renewed determination, Sam approached her.

"Cassie, we need to talk."

She'd heard Sam's voice so often in her dreams lately that at first it didn't register that he was really standing beside her. She'd only had eight hours' sleep in the past three days and was running on sheer adrenaline and caffeine. Now she was ready to crash. She wasn't ready to fight with him and she told him so.

"I don't want to fight with you, either," Sam said. "I just want to talk to you. I'd rather we were alone, but if you'd rather, we can talk right here where Mr. and Mrs. Friedman can see and hear us.''

Sure enough, the older couple was heading down the sidewalk in their direction.

And so Cassie had Sam come upstairs to her apartment.

Once inside, Sam got right to the point. ''Al told me you came to my press conference when I first returned home to the States. And that you changed your appearance after that. And before you go thinking he betrayed your trust, you should know that I was coming to speak to you anyway, because there was just too much stuff that I didn't understand. I ran into Al on my way over here and he said something in passing about the press conference. I bullied the rest out of him. Anyway, is it true?''

''Yes.'' Cassie curled up on the couch, tucking her feet under her and keeping her eyes fixed on the colorful Jamaican bowl on her makeshift coffee table. That way she wouldn't look at Sam, wouldn't be tempted to reveal how much she'd missed him.

''Why didn't you tell me?''

''The right time never came. Then things got complicated and I didn't want you thinking that I'd changed my appearance to get your attention. You already had women throwing themselves at you, I didn't want you thinking I was another groupie.''

''You know what I think?'' Sam said. ''I think you were afraid.''

That got her attention. ''Of what?''

''Of letting me see the real Cassie Jones underneath the whiplash-blond Cassandra Jones you show everyone else. Come here.''

Taking her by the hand, Sam gently tugged her off

the couch and led her into the bathroom where he took a soft washcloth and dampened it with warm water.

"Are you making me a warm compress again? Because I don't have a migraine tonight."

"I'm glad to hear that." He cupped her chin in one big hand and slowly lifted the washcloth to her face.

Cassie was baffled by his behavior. If she wasn't so tired she'd have put up a Tough Chick fight and stood her ground instead of just standing there frozen while he tenderly wiped her makeup away.

"Are you wearing contacts?" he asked.

She nodded. They'd been killing her dry eyes all day.

"Take them off."

"Then I'll be blind as a bat."

"You have glasses, don't you? Where are they?" Sam asked.

"In my backpack."

He returned an instant later and handed her the tiny-framed smart-girl glasses. Turning her to face the mirror, he stood behind her, his hands on her shoulders, his intense gaze meeting hers in the mirror. "It's you I love. Not a whiplash blonde, not a Tough Chick, but you, the real you. The one who's never had a hero of her own to fight her dragons for her, even if those dragons are of her own making." His voice softened and his blue eyes turned dark with emotion. "I want to be the man you wake up with for the next fifty years. I want to be the man who makes you smile. I want to be the man who'll give you children of your own. I want to be your hero. I want to be your husband."

Cassie bit down hard on her lower lip and blinked away the tears as it hit her that Sam wasn't trying to be charming here. He was telling the truth. He really did love the real her. She could see it in his eyes, read it on his handsome, stubborn face.

But she still had questions. She turned to face him. "Why did you say you wouldn't be interested in me when you looked at my photo?"

"I didn't know that was you. I thought you were asking me if I'd be interested in another woman. After all, you'd just said you didn't want to be one of many women in my life. I didn't even look at the female in the aforementioned photograph," he admitted gruffly. "I already knew you were the only woman for me. The only one I wanted as my wife. The only one whose dragons I wanted to slay."

His words unlocked the frozen curse around her heart and the last of her thorny defenses came tumbling down.

Cassie threw herself into Sam's arms and both of them almost ended up in the bathtub. She'd never kissed him with her glasses on and it took her a second or two to adjust.

Somehow, she wasn't exactly sure how, they ended up on her red couch, Sam's body pressed against hers. In between kisses she promised that she'd help him fight any dragons he had.

He tenderly cupped her face in his large hands. "You've already helped with that."

"I have? How?"

"By making me think about my reasons for being a Marine. And only by questioning my motives was I able to reach the conclusion that while I may indeed have gone into the Marines because it was the easy thing to do, I want to *stay* in the Marines because it's what I want to do and not because of my family's expectations.''

''I'm worried about your family.''

''Because of our blockhead gene, you mean? The one Prudence told you about?''

She smiled and shook her head. ''No, I can deal with blockheads.'' Her smile faded. ''I meant, I'm worried that your family might not accept me.''

''Of course they will.'' He gently stroked her jaw-line with the backs of his fingers. ''They'll love you just as I do.''

''I'm not so sure—''

''I am. You have nothing to worry about.'' He brushed his thumb over her well-kissed lips. ''Remember when we talked about fairy tales and I told you that I thought you fit the role of Sleeping Beauty the best?''

''I'm no beauty,'' Cassie said self-consciously. Her face was completely devoid of makeup and she felt stripped of her defenses. Her glasses had long since been discarded, which meant that she had to keep Sam close or his features became fuzzy.

''Hey, this *my* fairy tale and you're my Sleeping Beauty, the only one for me. But me…well, I'm just a Marine,'' Sam ruefully confessed, ''not a fairy-tale prince. But if that's good enough for you—''

With tears in her eyes, Cassie placed her hand over his mouth and whispered, ''Honor, Courage, Commitment. Those Marine Corps values are what make you a prince in my eyes. The only one for me.''

Sam sealed her vow with a passionately devoted kiss that finally made her believe she'd found her own special hero and her own special happily-ever-after.

Epilogue

One month later...

"**I** can't believe we really did it," Cassie murmured.

"Believe it." Sam leaned forward to seductively nibble her lower lip before settling his mouth over hers for a kiss guaranteed to melt steel. "We really are married. You are my wife."

She cupped his cheek with her hand, her gold wedding band nestled beside her vintage Art Deco-style diamond engagement ring. "And you're my husband."

"Have I told you how much I love your wedding dress?"

"I wore it just for you." The white strapless satin gown was very similar in style to the body-skimming, full-length dress she'd worn when Sam had first brought her to the Willard for that fund-raiser. Instead of the black silk ribbon she'd worn around her neck that night, tonight she was wearing the gorgeous turquoise necklace Sam had given her from the world-famous Sleeping Beauty mine.

She'd left her hair down to softly curl around her shoulders, its natural color restored. She no longer needed the artificial confidence being a temporary whiplash blonde had provided her. Instead she'd learned to be comfortable in her own skin, finally at ease with who she was. The journey was an ongoing one, but Cassie was no longer haunted by doubts from her past.

"How are you enjoying married life so far?" Sam asked.

Cassie sat back and surveyed the ballroom at Washington's prestigious Willard Hotel where their reception was being held. How could she ever have guessed when she'd come here to that black-tie fund-raiser with Sam that she'd end up returning here as his wife?

Then as now, tiny red, white and blue lights gleamed from white pillars set around the outer walls. Sam had requested them as a special reminder of the first time they'd come here. So much had changed since that night. Yet some things were still the same. Mrs. Friedman was still an avid gossip as she talked her husband's ear off before waving at Cassie from their table. Cassie's editor Phil was still fighting off nicotine cravings and Al was still creating magic with his camera. He'd also walked Cassie down the aisle and looked as proud as any real father could have been.

A majority of the ballroom was filled with Marines in dress blues. But there was only one Marine that interested her. Cassie touched his arm. "I'm loving married life."

"I wanted you to feel like a princess today," Sam

said, tenderly brushing his fingertips over her hand, which he'd held nonstop since she'd joined him in front of the minister.

"A princess, huh?" She slid her fingers between his, delighting in the sensual friction. "Because of my supposed Sleeping Beauty persona, right?"

Sam nodded.

"You do know that you're the only person on the face of the earth who thinks of me that way."

"Affirmative. And that's the way I like it." Sam's voice turned low and husky. "Knowing you as no one else ever has. Loving you as no one else ever will."

Emotion tightened her throat. Cassie loved him so much that it frightened her sometimes. But there was no doubt in her mind that she was meant to spend her life with Sam.

Pulling off a wedding like this in only four weeks hadn't been easy. But everything had gone so smoothly. Of course, she couldn't have managed without the acceptance and assistance of Sam's family. They'd taken her under their collective wing as if she'd always been one of them.

The feeling of belonging was still a new one for her, but one that filled her soul with happiness. Mrs. Wilder in particular had gone out of her way to provide Cassie with some much-needed maternal moral support. Cassie blinked away the sudden dampness from her eyes at the memory of how Sam's mother had stepped in to fill that role. After years of fending for herself, Cassie finally had a family of her own.

"Time to cut the cake, you two lovebirds," Joe called. "Or I could just have Matt here do it." He shifted the baby on his shoulder. "Matt has a thing for cakes, don't you, buddy?"

Cassie grinned, remembering Matt's food-tossing tendencies.

"Don't even think about it," Mrs. Wilder warned him.

"Vanessa is eating for two so she'll need a really big piece," Mark said, his voice reflecting his pride in his wife's pregnancy.

"Make me sound like a pig, why don't you?" Vanessa grumbled, socking Mark's arm with loving exasperation.

"You're a gorgeous princess," Mark replied, kissing her.

"There's enough romance in the air around here to choke a horse," Sam's oldest brother Justice proclaimed.

"Oh, sweetie." His wife Kelly placed one hand on her heart and sighed before flashing him a teasing grin. "You have such a way with words."

"Actions speak louder than words," Justice said before snaring her in his arms and kissing her.

"I can't believe this day has finally come." Mrs. Wilder leaned back and rested her head against her husband's shoulder. "All four of our sons happily married. I couldn't have picked better wives for them myself."

"I sure know that I couldn't have picked a better wife for *myself*," Bill Wilder gruffly stated, pulling her closer. "And I'd say we raised four impressive rough-tough-can't-get-enough Marines."

Cassie watched this all unfold before her eyes as she and Sam made their way to the multitiered cake. "You know I love you," she whispered to Sam. "But I really married you for your family."

Sam smiled. "Yes, I know."

"Okay, everyone, time for another photo op," Al declared, holding his digital camera. "Remember, I don't want any overly posed shots here. Look natural."

Baby Matt took Al at his word, reaching over and grabbing a handful of cake which he smeared across his face in his eagerness to eat it. Al captured the moment, and the ensuing laughter.

But it was the throwing of the bouquet that was the biggest surprise of the evening. All of Cassie's bridesmaids were her sisters-in-law and married to Wilder men so they couldn't stand in the small group of single women vying to catch the coveted bouquet.

Encouraged by their cheers, Cassie turned her back to the crowd and threw the bouquet. She didn't understand the hoots and shouted *ooohrahs!* of the Marines until she pivoted to see who had caught the flowers.

Striker stood at the bar with a stunned expression on his face as he gazed down at the bouquet.

"Good thing that wasn't a grenade," Joe teased Striker.

"You're supposed to duck from anything incoming," Justice reminded his buddy before slapping him on the back.

"Looks like that means you're the next one getting married," Mark noted.

Striker's stunned expression turned horrified.

Sam turned to Cassie and shook his head in amazement. "I'm impressed. You've got quite an arm on you, darling wife."

"I'd rather have your arms around me, darling husband," she replied with a grin.

"Your wish is my command," Sam murmured.

As he kissed her once again, Cassie couldn't help thinking that even Sleeping Beauty herself couldn't have been happier than Cassie was at that very moment. Sometimes fairy tales really did come true, even for supposedly Tough Chicks like herself.

*   *   *   *   *

SILHOUETTE *Romance*®

THE THUNDER CLAN

A family of proud, passionate people!

You've read brothers Nathan's and Grey's stories...
now read about their cousin, brooding black-sheep-by-
choice Conner, in THUNDER IN THE NIGHT (SR #1647),
coming in February 2003, only from
Donna Clayton and Silhouette Romance!

Nathan's story:
THE SHERIFF'S 6-YEAR-OLD SECRET
(SR #1623)

Grey's story:
THE DOCTOR'S PREGNANT PROPOSAL
(SR #1635)

Conner's story:
THUNDER IN THE NIGHT
(SR #1647)

Available at your favorite retail outlet.

Silhouette®
Where love comes alive™

Visit Silhouette at www.eHarlequin.com   SRTC2

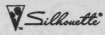

SPECIAL EDITION™

From *USA TODAY* bestselling author

SHERRYL WOODS

comes the continuation of the heartwarming series

Coming in January 2003
MICHAEL'S DISCOVERY
Silhouette Special Edition #1513

An injury received in the line of duty left ex-navy SEAL Michael Devaney bitter and withdrawn. But Michael hadn't counted on beautiful physical therapist Kelly Andrews's healing powers. Kelly's gentle touch mended his wounds, warmed his heart and rekindled his belief in the power of love.

Look for more Devaneys coming in July and August 2003, only from Silhouette Special Edition.

Available at your favorite retail outlet.

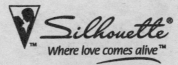

Where love comes alive™

Silhouette Romance presents tales of
enchanted love and things beyond explanation
in the heartwarming series

Soulmates

Couples destined for each other are brought
together by the powerful magic of love....

Broken hearts are healed

WITH ONE TOUCH

by Karen Rose Smith (on sale January 2003)

Love comes full circle when

CUPID JONES GETS MARRIED

by DeAnna Talcott (on sale February 2003)

Soulmates

Some things are meant to be....

*Available at
your favorite retail outlet.*

Where love comes alive™

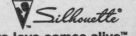

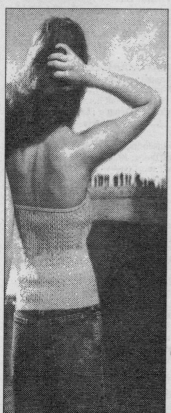

COMING NEXT MONTH

#1642 DUDE RANCH BRIDE—Madeline Baker

Ethan Stormwalker couldn't believe his eyes—the former love of his life
had arrived at his family's ranch in a bridal gown…without a groom! Defy-
ing her father's wishes, Cindy Wagner had fled an arranged marriage. Now
Cindy had to convince Ethan the only marriage she wanted arranged was to
him!

#1643 PRINCESS TAKES A HOLIDAY—Elizabeth Harbison

Princess Teresa of Corsaria wanted a break from the spotlight—she never
intended to be hit by a car! Sexy small-town doctor Dylan Parker kept her
secret while "Tess" healed. But when the truth about her identity came
out, would she choose the royal lifestyle over Dylan's TLC?

#1644 WHAT IF I'M PREGNANT…?—Carla Cassidy

The Pregnancy Test

Unmarried, successful and artificially inseminated, Colette Carson
thought a baby would fulfill her—until Tanner Rothman showed up!
Unsure of her pregnancy—and Tanner's reaction—she kept quiet about
her trip to the sperm bank. But if she *was* pregnant, would Tanner accept
her and another man's child?

#1645 IF THE STICK TURNS PINK…—Carla Cassidy

The Pregnancy Test

Bailey Jenkins was baby-hungry Melanie Watters's best friend—and the
perfect candidate for a father. Although Bailey wasn't interested in being
a dad, he agreed to a temporary marriage of convenience. But when the
stick finally turned pink, would he be able to let Melanie—and his
baby—go?

#1646 CUPID JONES GETS MARRIED—DeAnna Talcott

Soulmates

Cupid Jones had been helping the people of Valentine, Kansas, find true
love for years, but she'd just accidentally matched Burke Riley's mail-
order bride with another man! She volunteered herself as a replacement—
even though she could lose her special gift. Would her own marriage end
her matchmaking days or prove the best match of them all?

#1647 THUNDER IN THE NIGHT—Donna Clayton

The Thunder Clan

Conner Thunder returned to Smoke Valley Reservation to confront his
nightmares, not fall in love with Mattie Russell. But Mattie led a secret
life—a life Conner didn't understand. Now Conner must face his own
secrets in order to keep Mattie in his life—in his arms!—for good.

SRCNM0103